A BROOKHAVEN PARANORMAL COZY MYSTERY
BOOK 1

HIGH NOON

S.E. BIGLOW

For information contact; www.sarah-biglow.com

Edited by Under Wraps Publishing

Cover Design by: Deranged Doctor Design

Print ISBN: 978-1-955988-13-1

Published by S.E. Biglow: February 2022

10 9 8 7 6 5 4 3 2 1

For Grandma

April 28, 1927-January 4, 2022

Thank you for always being my biggest fan.

1

For the first time in weeks, I finally felt able to breathe. Leaving England had been the right decision, but it didn't make it any easier knowing the people I was leaving behind didn't fully understand why I had to go. Magic was in my blood. That much had become clear to me since my first time in the tiny oceanside town of Brookhaven, Massachusetts two months ago. But in London, I wasn't free to be myself. When I'd shared the news of my recently emerged magic with my parents, they'd told me I was a mental case.

Even though I'd seen what the start of my magic could do on my first trip to Brookhaven, the moment I'd set foot back on British soil, it was like that taste of power had vanished. I knew it wasn't really gone.

But being back home under my parents' scrutiny had stifled my progress. With no one to guide me, my magic was withering like an untended flower. I deserved to blossom and flourish.

My first visit to Brookhaven had been brief, but memorable. On my first night there, my host, Tania, and I wound up in the middle of a hit-and-run that turned out to be a robbery from High Time, the town's marijuana dispensary. I'd managed to harness my magic and it guided me to the culprit. Most sane people would have run the other direction after an experience like that. It had only drawn me closer. The feeling of safety I'd felt in the tiny town despite the danger was exactly what I needed. That and the people waiting to help me hone my skills like Tania, and the town's resident healer, Maggie.

Which was why I sat in the backseat of the cab, the boot—trunk as Americans called it—stuffed full of suitcases of clothes and other personal effects as it pulled up to a quaint little bed and breakfast bearing the name Tia Tania's in Brookhaven. I'd barely paid the cabbie when an older woman with graying hair raced out the front door.

"Darcy, we've been waiting for you," the eponymous Tania called.

"Sorry, my flight got delayed," I apologized and let the older woman wrap me in a tight embrace.

Tania Alvarez ran the bed and breakfast, and was the one to push me to explore my newly revealed magic when I'd come to stay for holiday two months ago. She'd insisted that when I made the decision to move here, that I stay with her as long as necessary. For a modest rent, of course.

"Beau's been positively glum without you," Tania rambled, pulling cases and bags out of the boot, and hefting them past the wooden sign with its red and purples roses.

Beau was a curious little fellow. A chameleon with telepathic tendencies who for some reason had taken a liking to me on my last visit. Communing with a non-verbal sentient creature had not been on my bucket list, but then neither had magic.

"I've missed him, too," I replied, following Tania inside and up toward the second floor. My gaze stopped halfway up on the banister where I'd first encountered Beau. The wood was smooth as I ran a hand along it. No chameleon hiding in plain sight today.

"I've left the room just as you had it," Tania said, nudging the bedroom door marked '4' open with her foot.

"I'm sure you've had plenty of people come through," I said and stepped in behind her. "But it is good to be back. Silly as it sounds, this already feels like home."

"I'm just glad to have a familiar face around again," she said and patted my shoulder.

She left me to settle in. Unlike my last visit, I took the time to unpack, filling the dresser neatly with shirts and undergarments. She'd provided empty hangers in the closet for trousers. The tiny hairs on the nape of my neck bristled as I stowed the now empty luggage in the back of the closet. I stood, pivoting slowly to find Beau perched on my pillow, blending in with the navy pillowcase. The curling of his tail and his slow blinking eyes were all that gave him away.

His sudden appearance would have freaked me out if he hadn't already done it to me before. In fact, the first time he'd appeared out of nowhere had been in this very room. Right before we'd gone off in search of a thief who'd nearly totaled Tania's car in their getaway. I didn't entirely understand how Beau's magic worked. But it didn't hurt that he could somehow extend his camouflage and invisibility powers to me when he felt like it. I settled on the bed and stroked one finger along his back.

"Heard you missed me, mate."

'*Happy now.*'

His soft voice echoed in my mind, and I couldn't help smiling. I glanced around, half expecting the B&B's other resident supernatural to make an appearance, but nothing happened.

'*Not here.*'

Well, that answered that question. The jet lag from the long flight—plus two stopovers—had caught up to me. I curled up on the bed, Beau settling against my shoulder.

I only intended to sleep for a little while, maybe an hour at most. I was sure Tania would wake me for supper. But when I finally woke, the sky outside was a deep inky blue and the clock on the night table read 12:10.

Part of me wanted to go back to sleep, but my empty belly rumbled, demanding food. Padding down the hall to the stairs, I took them as quickly and quietly as I dared down into the large, homey kitchen. A dim light on the oven's display caught my eye and in the pale moonlight I found the note Tania had left.

Leftovers in the oven when you want them.

Realizing that fumbling in the dark in a still-unfamiliar space was a recipe for disaster, I turned on the light above the stove and rummaged in the cabinets for a plate and some utensils. The scent of lasagna wafted at me as I pulled out the foil wrapped leftovers.

"Oh, you're back," a snarky tenor voice said from behind me.

"Leave it to a ghost to come lurking after midnight," I answered and took a forkful of pasta before facing Sam, the establishment's resident ghost.

He appeared even more flamboyantly dressed than the last time I'd encountered him, which seemed impossible given that when last we'd met, he'd worn sequins. He was dead, but I'd never asked him how he could change his outfit. It had seemed unimportant at the time to ask. I had barely scratched the surface of how magic and ghosts worked in my short time in Brookhaven. All I'd really learned was this was a safe place for me to learn to use and hone my magic.

"I can't just sit around all day, hoping some perky British chick with a fondness for plants walks in," he quipped.

"I am not perky," I argued in spite of myself.

Sam gave me an exaggerated wink and gestured toward my torso. "Anyway," he drew out the start of the word for dramatic effect and added, "It's a good thing you did come back. I was starting to worry Tania would have to move."

The fork fell out of my hands. "What? Why would she have to do that?"

"In case you haven't noticed, we aren't exactly swimming in guests."

"Yeah, but I'm sure you will. A place like this must do brilliant come Halloween time. After my visit, I read online it's like one giant spooky festival all of October."

"We're no Salem," he sighed. "Point is, it's good you're here, so at least Tania's got someone bringing in some steady cash."

"Well, after what she did for me, I'm grateful to her for letting me stay."

Sam fluttered closer, propped his chin in his hand and batted his lashes. "And I'll have you know, Ginny Hayes has been all aflutter about your return, too."

"Why does she care?" Ginny was Brookhaven's resident gossip and for some reason I had yet to discern, people still listened to her. She ruled the roost at the local coffee shop on Main Street. She'd been partly responsible for my new boss, Sage, being questioned by police about the theft during my first visit here. Ginny had given me the idea that the dispensary proprietor had stolen from her own till. A lie, but one I'd repeated to the town's Chief of Police. I'd had my share of blame for it, too, but surely she'd moved on in the months since I'd been gone.

"Because you're new and exciting, and Sage won't shut up about you. She keeps calling you her miracle grower."

"Bloody hell." I'd been offered a job at the town's dispensary tending to the crop since their last grower, in cahoots with his uncle in Town Hall, had in fact been the one to commit the theft. I haven't even had my first day on the job yet. I had received an official offer letter from High Time to secure my green card, but that was all.

"How has Sage been managing?" I probed around another bite of pasta.

"From what I've heard, she's had to cover the plant tending duties herself for the last two months." He flashed me a smirk. "You made waves and it hasn't gone unnoticed, is all I'm saying."

I didn't want to be the talk of the town. I just wanted to blend in with the rest of the town's population where I could learn to harness my powers in peace. I didn't need the town gossip speculating about me. Not when her brother was the Chief of Police, and he wasn't very fond of me.

I finished my leftovers in silence, set the plate and utensils in the sink to soak, and retreated to my room. Beau was nowhere to be seen when I returned. My mind and body were at war, telling me I was meant to be starting my day now. I forced myself to curl up beneath the blankets and nestle my head against the pillow, letting the comfortable bed lull me back to sleep.

A KNOCK AT THE DOOR ROUSED ME THE SECOND TIME and I sat up to see early morning summer sun streaming in through the windows. Tania stuck her head in and gave me a grin.

"Nervous for your first day?" Her tone carried a touch of anxiety that I wasn't entirely certain was her own.

"A little," I answered and climbed out of bed.

"You're going to do great," she said, her Spanish accent coming through heavier on the last word.

I appreciated her vote of confidence as I showered and dressed for my first day of work at High Time. It still amazed me that even though I'd accused the owner of stealing from her own till months ago, she'd turned around and offered me a job. Tania's sway in town hadn't hurt matters, either.

"You seem cheerful," I noted as Tania passed me a travel mug of coffee and a muffin.

"Oh, I just have a good feeling about today," she answered with a one-shouldered shrug.

From what little I knew of my landlady, she was a witch like me, but her magic leaned more toward emotion. She called herself an empath. Except the way she often knew things before they were going to happen made me wonder if she had some form of precognition, even if she wasn't fully aware of it.

"I don't start my shift for a little bit, maybe we could have a chat first," I said, sliding into the chair I'd occupied a few hours earlier. The kitchen was far brighter and cheerier in daylight.

"Something on your mind?" Tania sat across from me.

"Well, I know I just got here and all, but I was hoping we could start working on my magical ... education?" I took a sip of coffee.

"I suppose it's never too early to learn something new," she mused. "Where do you want to start?"

"How does magic actually work? Like, if we're both witches, why do we do different things?"

She leaned back in her chair. "Well, I'm not an expert. But from what I was taught, magic manifests most often in bloodlines from two camps. Those connected to the elements and those linked to humanity."

"So, like your ability to sense feelings," I noted.

"Yes. And I suspect your hedge witch abilities are linked to the element of earth."

"I suppose that makes sense." I took another sip of coffee. "What about ghosts? How does that all work? I mean I've only met Sam, but there must be loads of others around?"

"Ghosts are a difficult topic. One I think we should keep for another time. Besides, you don't want to be late."

My mind raced as I walked the short trek up Main Street to the dispensary with its light-up sign of a sneaker with a marijuana leaf at its center. Customers already congregated outside, waiting for the shop to open up. I was hopeful that many of them would become familiar faces in time. An older gentleman at the front of the queue looked familiar. *Hadn't he been here when I first met Sage?*

I was about to join the line, not having an official employee ID badge to get into the building on my own, when tires crunched on the gravel behind me. I turned to see Sage pull into the parking spot labeled Owner. Her car had been serviced since last we'd seen each other in person.

She was a spunky woman with aqua colored hair that matched her eyes, accented by trendy glasses. She climbed out of the driver's seat and gave me a wave.

"Come on around the back Darcy," Sage called.

I left the line behind and joined her at the back door. She led me through the large kitchen, where staff was already busy baking confections and other edible treats, to the grow room.

"How's business been?" I asked, trying to make light conversation as I waited for Sage to give me directions.

"Great, actually." She leaned in close. "I think some folks took pity on me with the whole robbery thing and were trying to throw some extra business my way."

"I noticed a Help Wanted sign in the front window," I said as she handed me a lanyard with an ID badge.

"Yeah, we're looking for some more folks to run the registers out front." She gestured to the ID badge. "This one's just a temporary one. It will get you around the building until I have a chance to take your picture."

"Thanks." I looked around at the carefully temperature-controlled room with its grow lights and ample spacing for plants to flourish. It had to have been my mind playing tricks on me, but the plants were quiet since I'd gone back to London. My magic, as far as I could tell, involved plants reaching out to me in their limited sentience, whispering the promise of what they could be to guide me. I'd come to Brookhaven looking for an escape from it, only to find that this was just where I needed to get a handle on my powers.

Tania might have magic, and Sam might be a ghost, but that didn't mean everyone in town was fully aware of the supernatural. To my knowledge, Sage just thought I had a way with plants—a normal, run-of-the-mill green thumb. I had to hope I didn't disappoint her.

"Why don't I give you the penny tour?" Sage offered before I could settle in.

"Sounds great."

"Well, obviously this is the grow room. It's where all the magic happens."

I gaped at her. Had my assumption been off base about her not knowing about magic? "Not the first person I've heard say that. Is there something I should know?"

"Just a figure of speech," she said, dismissing my question.

She ushered me back to the kitchen. "This the kitchen crew. That's Thomas, he's our head baker," she said, pointing to a tall lanky guy in an apron.

He waved before turning back to the task at hand. She gestured to another door. "That's the employee break area. And my office is just through there."

I tried to make a mental map of the small space. It wouldn't be hard to remember. "Think I've got it. And out front is obviously where the sales happen."

"You got it," she said with a smile. "Now, we cultivate fresh leaves every week or two. Though it's been a bit spotty the last month or so," she continued. "You'll want to make sure you're taking extra care."

"Right, yeah. And um ... I know it's going to sound silly, but what exactly am I supposed to do with the plants?'

"Make sure the grow lights are calibrated properly and nudge along any plants that seem to be lagging."

The way she talked made me think she did know more about me and my powers than she was letting on. "I'll let you get comfortable," Sage called before disappearing through the break room and into her office.

I left the kitchen behind and tried not to panic as I stood there, in the middle of the room, surrounded by plants all starting to notice my presence. One by one they started tickling my magical senses.

"Not today. I'm not ready," I said.

I would learn to control and harness my magic. Though not today, I wanted to be a normal woman on her first day in a new job. I wanted to learn all the company rules and fill out all the boring forms. I wasn't ready for magic to take hold and push itself on me. I still didn't entirely know how my magic worked and until Tania had time to teach me, I didn't want to risk testing my limits and ruining Sage's new crop of plants.

Thankfully, by the time lunch rolled around, Sage had returned with a stack of forms. I was able to sit and focus on those, instead of the plants surrounding me. A little after noon, I found Sage in the back office and handed over my completed forms.

"Great," she said, flipping through them. "Oh, I need your work authorization before we can actually get you on payroll," she said.

My passport and work authorization card were still sitting in my travel bag back at Tania's. I'd been in such a rush to get to the shop on time, I hadn't even considered bringing them along. "Right, of course," I apologized. "I can run and get them now. I'll be back in ten minutes."

"Why don't you take this as your lunch break and just bring them when you come back."

I wanted to tell her that I hadn't done anything strenuous enough to require a break, but arguing with my boss on the first day wasn't going to make a good impression. So, I accepted her generosity and retreated to the bed and breakfast. Tania stood in the kitchen pouring a handful of beans into a large pot.

"I wasn't expecting you back for lunch," she called as I started up the stairs.

"Forgot some things in my bag," I answered and took the stairs two at a time.

Someone had stacked my passport and work card on the night table by the clock. I would have guessed it was Sam if he'd been corporeal, or Beau if he could read, but neither option seemed plausible. Or maybe Tania's powers had kicked in and she knew I'd left the documents behind and needed to find them in a hurry? I checked my bag and found my wallet still there with all of my other ID and a handful of pound notes I hadn't changed over to American currency yet. Everything appeared to be in order, so I scooped up the identification, shoving them in my back pocket.

I was halfway down the stairs when the doorbell rang.

"Darcy, would you mind getting that?" Tania called from the kitchen.

I descended the final few steps and pulled open the door. A young woman with poorly dyed brown hair stood on the front step clutching a duffel bag.

"Can I help you?" I asked before realizing it wasn't my place. "Actually, I don't work here. Let me get the owner."

"I'm looking for a place to stay."

"Come in, come in. We've got plenty of room," Tania said, her voice so close behind me that I jumped.

My host's penchant for knowing when people would be arriving on her doorstep was definitely a sign she was hiding more than just her empathic abilities. As I stepped aside to let the young woman in, I couldn't help but feel a new wave of nerves. Just like this morning, I wasn't sure it was my own emotion.

2

The young woman looked shell-shocked by Tania's insistence that there were available rooms. Maybe she'd been expecting the B&B to be full up. Not that there were any other hotels in town to compete.

"There's a room at the top of the stairs, number 2. You can leave your bags up there," Tania said, gesturing to the staircase.

"I'm not sure I caught your name," I said as the young woman stepped over the threshold and into the front hall, bag gripped tight in her fingers.

"Vera. Vera Chase," she answered without making eye contact.

"Nice to meet you. I'm Darcy. I'm also staying here," I said and held out a hand for her to shake.

She didn't respond, instead she scurried up the stairs out of sight. I retreated to the kitchen to find Tania tending to the pot on the stove. I inhaled and caught the scent of chilies. She didn't say a word as I stood there watching her work. "This is good news right? Another boarder?"

"It is. Although, by the emotions rolling off her, I'm not sure how long she's going to stay," Tania answered.

It also meant I didn't know how long we'd have to keep our conversations about magic quiet. We didn't need to scare Vera off.

My stomach rumbled with hunger as I realized I'd already wasted half of my lunch break. I gestured to the pot on the stove. "Is that going to be ready soon?"

"Sorry, it still needs to simmer for a while."

That left Ginny's Coffee Clutch at the heart of town. They had decent coffee and sandwiches, but it also came with some less desirable fixtures. Like Ginny Hayes holding court at the counter, her signature white, blonde hair done up in a high bun as I walked in. I hadn't put it together before. Though I supposed Ginny was always present, because she owned the place. I'd let Ginny's gossip steer me wrong about the theft from High Time two months ago. I wasn't eager to be on her radar again.

Her seat swiveled as the door closed behind me, the sound of the tiny bell overhead still ringing out my arrival. Her gaze narrowed ever so slightly when it met mine. I tried not to acknowledge her, but it seemed everyone else's attention had fallen on us and I had no choice. So, I gave her a small wordless nod and headed for a seat at the end of the counter.

"Welcome back," a young man with eerily similar coloring to Ginny greeted.

"You remembered," I replied, trying to recall his name and not seem too obvious as I glanced at his name placard.

Marco.

"Well, you are very memorable," he said, a blush creeping onto his cheeks.

Lord, is he flirting with me?

He cleared his throat, held up his notepad and asked, "What can I get you?"

"Uh, just a coffee and a roast beef on wheat to go, if you don't mind."

He didn't even bother jotting it down as he gave me a confident smile and retreated to the window into the kitchen, calling out my order. I did my best to not attract attention as I waited for my food. The bell above the front door tinkled, announcing someone's entrance and, before I realized it, I was spinning in my seat. I spotted Tania guiding Vera to a table in the back of the café. Marco materialized as soon as they slid into their seats, pen poised to jot down notes.

Everyone in this town can't be magical, could they?

"Order up!" one of the cooks called, slamming his fist down on a bell that gave a half-hearted rattle from having been hit so vigorously. Tania caught me watching and she waved a hand, summoning me over.

"I'm actually going to join them and eat here," I told Marco as he darted past me to the kitchen.

"You got it." He carried my coffee and sandwich behind me as I went to join my host and new housemate.

"I was going to grab and go, but I can sit for a few minutes," I said.

"Vera was just telling me that she's come to Brookhaven looking for a fresh start," Tania said in a soft tone.

Fresh starts seemed to be the order of the day at Tania's B&B. Marco returned in short order with drinks and Vera turned her attention to sucking down as much of the water as she could. There were so many questions I wanted to ask her about what had led her to this little seaside haven. Was she, like me, looking to learn a craft or had something more mundane drawn her here? She seemed so nervous and on edge. Her gaze kept darting around the establishment, landing in one place for a few seconds before moving on to someone else. It seemed like she was people watching. I caught her looking at Ginny more than once. Ginny was deep in conversation with the people on either side of her. Her interest in my arrival was apparently short-lived.

"So, Vera, what drew you to Brookhaven, other than wanting to start over?" I asked, hoping to drum up some conversation in the few minutes I had before I needed to get back to work.

"Nothing, really," she replied.

"I'm pretty new around here, too. I came here on holiday a few months ago and it just felt like the place I needed to be."

"I just needed a change from the city," Vera offered, hands clutched around the water cup in front of her. "I just went to the bus station and found one going as far as I could get."

"Well, Brookhaven is a safe place. It's in the name," Tania interjected with a soft laugh.

"I don't want to speak for Tania, but I'm sure

she'd love to show you the sights. She can be quite the knowledgeable tour guide," I said.

"I could do with getting out for a while," Tania agreed.

"I'm not much into sightseeing," Vera replied. Her gaze drifted across the café, and she turned so her back faced that side of the room. "But, uh, I could use a job."

I glanced the direction she'd turned, but didn't spot anything that would account for her nerves.

"What sort of job?" Tania voiced, pulling me out of my own head.

Before coming here, I hadn't believed in things like fate. But after I'd found myself in the thick of a mystery that my unique power helped to solve, I wasn't so eager to dismiss the notion out of hand. Maybe that was why I felt drawn to this young woman. Maybe we had both been put in this place at the same time for a reason.

"I might be able to help with that," I said. "At least, I know someone who is hiring."

Vera's head perked up and she met my gaze for the first time since I'd joined their table. She smiled at me and it brightened up her pale features. "I'll take whatever I can find. Thanks."

Across the café, silverware clattered to the floor,

drawing the room's collective attention long enough to see Marco bending down near one of the tables by the window. A man sat with his back to us, but I could make out a scruffy beard in his reflection. A shiver danced down my spine as he turned toward us. I'd never seen him before, but the weight of his gaze made me uncomfortable. I averted my gaze and focused on my food, suddenly remembering I needed to get back on the clock.

"Normally you are not such a butter fingers, Marco," Tania said when he brought her and Vera's meals.

"Everyone has an off day, Tia," he answered sharply before disappearing into the employee area of the cafe.

"That was a little harsh of you," I commented around a bite of beef.

"Oh, I've opened my big mouth, haven't I? I didn't mean to be critical. It was more I could tell it had frustrated him and I spoke without thinking." She tapped her temple when she noted the frustration, leading me to assume she meant she'd sensed his emotion.

The fact that Tania, with her at least two decades more life experience than me, had trouble reining in her powers made me nervous. I'd thought she had it all together when we first met. I'd assumed that's why she'd offered to help me learn to control my plant magic.

Before I could speak, Ginny's obviously loud tone carried across the café, drawing my attention. I couldn't see who she was speaking to, but whoever they were, they were leaning in close, rapt in her attention.

"Our little town doesn't see a lot of new faces, so when they show up, it's memorable," Ginny blathered. The grind of the stool swiveling to face me made my teeth ache. "It does seem as if they like to congregate."

"No one asked your opinion, Ginny," Marco said loudly, coming to refill Vera's water.

"I'll have you know plenty of people value my opinion here," Ginny retorted. "At least I have a respectable job. Instead of being a glorified gardener at the dispensary."

"There's a dispensary? Is it controversial or something?" Vera asked.

"Don't let her fool you. She's got her hands in the dispensary, too," Tania murmured.

"She just doesn't like me for some reason," I added. "As for the dispensary, it's only my first day.

But the staff are friendly and the boss is willing to take chances on new people."

"Sage is the forgiving sort," Tania agreed. "After all, she hired Darcy here after a little misunderstanding."

Vera arched a brow at me. "What happened?"

I ducked my head in embarrassment. "I may have accidentally accused her of stealing money from her own till. It made sense to me at the time based on the information I had. Turned out I was wrong."

"What, were you like a cop in another life?"

"No. Definitely not. But I felt a certain responsibility to figure out what happened."

Tania smiled. "I'll fill you in later." She tapped her watch and looked at me. "I've kept you longer than I should have. You should get back to work." She turned to Vera. "And I believe you have a job to apply for."

I tossed a couple of bills on the table to cover my meal. Standing, I checked my pocket to make sure I had the documents Sage still needed for my file and Vera followed me out of Ginny's. I caught her looking back over her shoulder as the door swung shut behind us. I followed the direction of her gaze and saw the bearded man still sitting at his table by the window.

"Do you know that guy?" I led the way across Main Street and up half a block back to High Time.

"No."

The energy that infused her demeanor moments ago vanished again and she retreated into her shell. Maybe suggesting she apply for the front desk position at the shop wasn't the brightest idea I'd had after all. Not if she could be so mercurial. But it wasn't my decision whether or not to hire her.

"Just wait here a minute," I said and gestured to the front of the shop before I used my temporary ID to buzz into the grow room.

I hadn't expected for the plants to perk up at my approach. They'd quieted down this morning and yet, they were abuzz, taking notice of my entry into their space again. I could hear their promises of what they might one day become. The help they might offer to those in need. I could even sense a strange undercurrent of what I might one day use them for to cast a spell.

That's new.

I'd spent so much time denying my magic and pretending it would go away, I hadn't allowed myself the chance to figure out just what I could do when I set my mind to it. And aside from hunting down the thief who'd stolen money from the dispensary while on holiday, I hadn't had cause to use my skills.

"You're late," Sage's voice interrupted my musing.

"Sorry. I know that's a really bad thing on your first day. I swear, it won't happen again. But I think the reason I'm a bit late might make up for it." I rambled.

"And what reason is that?"

"I found someone looking for a job, who might be a good fit for the front counter."

"You just happened to stumble across someone willing to sell pot to small town hippies? What, did they materialize out of thin air by magic?"

She may very well have.

"There's a new boarder at Tania's and she's looking for work."

Sage tapped the edge of her phone against her chest. "You think she'd be good?"

"Well, honestly, I don't know much about her, but I assumed you'd be able to judge whether she'd be any good. She's out front right now. Name's Vera."

Sage nodded and set her phone on the desk beside her. "What's your take on her? Give me your honest opinion."

"She's a bit shy. But there could be loads of

reasons. She is in a new place, coming from the city. She's probably used to a faster paced way of life. Lord knows I was. But she seems like a decent person. Not that it's my decision or anything, but I'd give her a chance."

Sage pushed her glasses up the bridge of her nose. "Well, I wasn't going to fill it with any of the locals anyway."

I wanted to push her on that, but I didn't need to be an empath to sense she was still feeling burned by the fact that one of her star employees had betrayed her trust. Someone she'd considered a friend.

I tugged the work card and passport from my back pocket. "Oh, and I brought these."

She accepted them and gestured for me to follow her. I trailed her to the back office where she made copies of my documents and pointed to a blank stretch of bare white wall. "Stand there and try to look like you're happy to be here."

Doing as she instructed, I straightened up to my full height and plastered on a big grin as she snapped a photo with her phone. "So, you aren't mad enough that I won't get my proper ID, then."

"I'll let you know how it goes," she said and

made her way to the front of the shop, leaving me to return to the grow room.

I knew Sage didn't expect magic or miracles from me tending her plants, but I felt I owed it to her to try anyway. So, I spent the next five hours talking to the plants. Encouraging them to grow. I thought one plant that looked a little wilted perked up slightly, but it also could have been the fact I moved it into more direct light.

I was emotionally drained by the time I returned to the B&B. The spicy scent of chili drew me to the kitchen where Tania stood dishing out three bowls along with thick slices of bread that smelled freshly baked.

"Well, how was your first day?" she asked, pushing a bowl my way.

"Tiring. But good." I looked around. "Where's Vera?"

"How do I look?" the young woman called from the entryway. I turned to find Vera wearing a brightly colored High Time shirt.

"Like you belong. Welcome to the team," I said with a broad grin.

3

We'd settled into a nice routine by the time Vera had been with us for a week. She only gave Tania and I the occasional side eye when one of us had to surreptitiously scold Sam for being cheeky.

"Do you think Sage would be mad if we called out today? It's so gross out," Vera sighed, staring out at the downpour through the back kitchen window.

"I think it is smarter to ask your co-worker for a ride," Tania replied, setting down a spatula.

"I'm all for driving there today," I started, setting my coffee cup on the counter, "but I don't think you want me driving. I'm still thrown off driving on the other side of the road."

"I think you can manage the trip. It's only two

turns," Tania said and pointed to the little rack affixed to the side of the refrigerator. "Take the car."

"Are you sure?" I probably should have mentioned I wasn't entirely certain my U.K. driver's license was applicable here. I hadn't had time to go and get a proper U.S. one yet.

"Lucky for me, my job is right here so I don't have to go outside in this weather. I won't miss it," she answered with a smile.

My phone beeped in my pocket, reminding me that if we didn't leave soon, we'd be late. Tossing back the last dregs of my coffee, I donned a jacket and plucked the keys from their spot on the rack. Vera followed suit and we both darted to Tania's little newer-model VW Bug in the drive. I let out a sigh as I pulled the car door shut, blocking out the hammering rain and whipping gusts of wind.

"I promise I will do my best to get us there in one piece." I adjusted the rearview mirror and nearly jumped as Sam flashed a grin before disappearing into the rain. His sparkly outfit completely unaffected by the downpour.

I can't believe I'm jealous of a ghost.

Someone was smiling down on me, because I managed the short trip without hydroplaning or hitting anything. And I even drove on the correct side of the road. Pulling into the back lot of High Time, I eased into the closest spot to the door, right next to Sage's car.

"Um, I think there might be an umbrella in the back," I said, twisting unsuccessfully to peer into the tiny backseat. Even from my limited vantage point, I didn't see anything there. Which meant if there was an umbrella it would be in the tiny boot at the back.

"I'll check the trunk," Vera replied and tugged the hood of her jacket up over her hair.

I should have gone with her, but it seemed foolish for both of us to end up soaked. I heard the latch on the back release and the boot lid appeared in the rearview mirror. I prepared myself for the mad dash into the back door of the shop as Vera came around with the hoped-for umbrella. She held it aloft as I braced myself and shouldered the door open, fighting against the wind. A gust threatened to render the umbrella useless as we raced side-by-side to the employee entrance.

Vera pawed at her pockets with one hand, trying to steady the umbrella with the other. "I forgot my ID. I thought I had it when we left, but now ..." She cast a look back at Tania's car.

I tugged the lanyard from under my jacket and buzzed us both in. "Don't worry about it."

We hurried inside; the door slamming shut behind us. Winding our way through the kitchen to the small employee break room, I hung my water-logged jacket on a peg beside the small row of lockers and did my best not to shiver.

"That's one hell of a storm we're having," Thomas commented, donning his apron. He wore his long dark hair in dreads, tied back into a tail which he finished shoving under a hair net.

"Really kills motivation," Vera replied before leaving Thomas and I alone.

"She's got a weird sense of humor, doesn't she?" he noted, before laughing as though he indeed found her statement funny.

As much as the solitude of the grow room allowed me to practice my magic, it was a bit lonely. Sure, Sage would pop in from time to time when new plants were ready to be harvested, but more often than not, it was just me and the plants.

"Okay, Darcy, you can do this," I said, sitting in front of a newly potted plant. It had just barely begun to poke through the soil in its bay. I'd decided I was going to see if I could encourage it to grow—with magic.

"Right, just feel the plant and what it wants to be," I murmured.

As Tania had explained, magic feels different for every person, just like we each have different skills. Though we're all connected by an intricate, unseen web of magic in the world. I just had to learn to tap into it and make it do what I wanted.

Easier said than done.

I started by cupping my hands around the pot and closing my eyes. I focused on the smell of the earth and the growing plants. The smells grounded me and connected me to every living thing in the room. Dozens of soft whispers bombarded my thoughts and I pulled my hands off the pot. I was casting too broad a net. I needed to focus on this specific plant and block out all the rest.

"Here goes nothing."

I gently pinched the stem of the plant between my right thumb and forefinger and closed my eyes again. It pulsed against the pads of my fingers, sending shivers of excitement down my spine. The mass of voices dwindled one by one until all I could hear was the plant in front of me. It trembled beneath my touch. It was ... *scared?*

"Uh, you don't have to be scared to grow. It's natural. It's what you're meant to do," I said, hoping I achieved an encouraging tone of voice.

The stem shrunk back, as if it could hide in the

dirt and return to the soil from which it had come. I pinched tighter out of instinct. That only drove the plant deeper into itself.

"Come on. You don't have to be afraid. I want to help you. Please, we both need this, okay?" I pleaded, opening my eyes and looking down at the shriveled seedling in my hands. "Look, you're going to grow one way or the other. And it would be really great if I could help you do it. I'm still pretty new to being a witch and I have never done this before. So, seeing you grow, because I helped would be a big boost to my confidence."

"Who are you talking to?" Vera's voice drifted in from the door leading to the front of the shop.

I broke contact with the plant and heat crept up my neck. I coughed to clear my throat which only made me look more conspicuous. "Nothing."

"You were talking to that plant like you could make it grow," she replied.

"A girl's got to find ways to amuse herself when she's just tending plants all day," I lied. As much as I liked Vera, she didn't need to be in the know about my secret. "Plus, I read an article that said talking to plants helps them grow."

"I heard you say you were a witch," she continued, gaze narrowed.

"It was a joke. Magic's not real," I said, hating every word coming out of my mouth. It was a lie I'd believed for too long. When my magic first appeared, my parents had denied its existence. Maybe if I'd been more open to my powers from the start, I'd be farther along in knowing how to use them.

"You think I'm stupid," Vera snarled, her mood taking a sharp turn without warning.

"No, I don't," I said, standing and taking a step toward her. She backed away and the door slammed shut behind her before I could make it past the first row of benches.

What was that about?

My hand moved to my front pocket to grab my phone and text Tania when I realized I'd left it in my locker in the break room. Vera's sudden mood change was odd, but it could wait until my lunch break. Besides, even though the seedling had been resistant, I thought I could feel a spark of interest from it. A little nugget of possibility for me to tease out over time.

Time passed slowly as I tried—and failed—to coax the seedling from the soil in its trench. The walls of the grow room were thicker than most, but sound still carried. I could hear the clatter of trays from the kitchen and the slamming of oven doors opening and closing. The voices of the kitchen staff were muffled by the other ambient noise. The front of the shop was a different story. Normally, it was quiet, even when people came in to pick up or place orders. But at a little before noon, according to the digital clock on the far wall, raised voices drew my attention to the front of the shop. And one of them was unmistakably Vera.

"You need to leave. Now."

"Please. I just need a moment," a tenor voice pleaded. "Kenz, please."

"I don't know who Kenz is. That isn't my name," Vera spat back. "And if you don't leave right now, I'm going to call the police."

There was a lull in the argument and then Vera's voice rose again. "Get out!"

I left the plants behind and pushed through the door into the area behind the counter. The door to the outside swung shut behind a male figure. "Everything okay?" The space was empty save for Vera at the far end of the counter. I had expected other people to come check on her, but no one came.

"Fine," she answered, but wouldn't look at me. Whoever she'd been speaking to had gotten the hint and left.

"That didn't sound fine," I pushed. "If you want to ask Sage if you can take a break, I can cover the front for you."

Vera spun, something crumpled in her hand. It looked like a napkin or a receipt, but she held it too tight to discern more detail. "Go back to your plants, Darcy. *Please.*"

The pleading in her voice as she said the last word urged me to stick close rather than let her be. My mind started to whirl as I eyed the space around us. There were cameras. We could ask Sage to go over the recording and pinpoint the man who'd upset her. If she felt threatened, she could give it to the police to ensure they made the right person stay away.

"I'm trying to help, Vera," I said. "I don't mean to intrude, but you look pretty shaken. I'm sure Sage won't mind you taking your break a few minutes early." I pointed to the front window. "Looks like the rain stopped. Maybe you should get some air."

Her shoulders hunched and then lowered. Her jaw relaxed and she nodded. "Okay. Yeah, maybe I'll do that."

I watched her go and turned to the counter, stepping up to the register. *Good move, Darcy.* Offering to watch the till was generous of me, except I didn't have the bloody code in the event anyone came in looking to make a purchase.

"There you are," Sage said, appearing at the counter next to me.

"Sorry, I should have told you I was stepping out. Vera had a bad interaction with a customer, so I offered to watch the front while she got some air," I explained. "I told her to check with you first, of course."

"She did. You should go get some lunch, too. Thanks for looking out for her", Sage said and patted my shoulder. "I've got it here."

I retreated back through the grow room to the employee break room. I found my phone and dialed Tania's number. It went to voicemail after four rings. I didn't bother leaving a message. Instead, I donned my jacket and made a quick trip to Ginny's. Thankfully, it wasn't crowded, and I could sit at the counter without getting stared at. To my surprise, Ginny wasn't around. Marco popped by to take my order and deposited it in front of me with a smile.

"Hey, can I ask you something?" I gripped the handle of my coffee mug.

"Sure," he answered.

"Ginny owns this place, right?"

"Her name's on the door," he replied.

"Yeah. But I've seen you give her lip and get away with it. How's that possible?"

"Pays to be the owner's cousin," he said with a one-shoulder shrug.

Well, that explained it. Tania had once told me the Hayes family was a big deal in Brookhaven. That seemed to still be true.

I checked the time and nearly choked on my sandwich. Lunch had again flown by. "Hey, Marco, can I get the coffee to go?" I called and gestured to my mug.

"Sure thing," he answered, seeming to be in better spirits today.

After making a quick trip to the restroom, I found my coffee waiting at my chair. I left him a larger than normal tip and headed back toward the dispensary. I downed half of the To-Go cup on the short walk back. Almost out of nowhere, a thrumming started behind my eyes and my stomach sloshed with nausea. *Something's off with the coffee.* I took a few deep breaths and made it back to the grow room before everything started to swim and went dark.

THE HALOGEN LIGHTS BUZZED ABOVE ME WHEN I CAME to. My to-go cup lay on the floor beside me, spilled coffee reaching all the way to the wall. How long had I been passed out? My head throbbed now as I pushed myself to a seated position. The clock on the wall read 2:07. I'd been on my way back shortly before 1:00. No one had come to check on me. *Because they didn't have a reason.* They were probably busy doing their own jobs. And Sage was focused on manning the till out front.

My stomach still sloshed as I got to my feet. Hurrying into the kitchen I found a cloth to sop up the spilled mess before going to look for Sage. She was still out front. That's odd. Vera should have been back by now.

"You look terrible," Sage noted as the customer she'd been assisting turned her back and shoved a little green package into her purse.

"I'm not feeling great, if I'm honest. I think something from lunch didn't agree with me. I hate to do this, but I think I need to take the rest of the shift off."

"Go home and get some rest. And when you see Vera, tell her she better not skip out on me again without notice. I get needing air, but it's not okay to bail without letting me know."

Retracing my steps to the break room, I stopped long enough to pick up the umbrella we'd borrowed from the car that morning. The weather had cleared, but it was the courteous thing to return it to its rightful spot. I eased into the driver seat, but my stomach finally got the better of me. I barely managed to make it to a rubbish bin at the back of the building before getting sick.

I wiped my mouth with the sleeve of my jacket and then my hands on my pants to get rid of the sweat. My entire body felt clammy as I returned to the car. The umbrella sat across the front seats. I tugged it free and tried to set it along the small back-seat when I noticed the hood of the boot blocking the view out the back window. If Vera hadn't shut it properly this morning, there could be water damage to the interior. A sense of foreboding washed over me like an unexpected wave as I rounded the car. My fingers trembled as I eased the lid open to reveal Vera's body crammed into the tight space, her unseeing gaze staring up at me.

4

It took my brain far too long to register what my eyes were seeing. I somehow managed to muffle a scream by shoving my fist into my mouth. *Why would Vera be in the boot?* My gaze moved from her face down to the length of something thick and green around her throat. I knew I should have paid more attention to what it was, but my brain was in overload. I could see the marks it had made on her skin. Part of me knew what I'd find if I pressed a finger to her neck, but I did it anyway. After all, there could be some chance she was still alive.

No pulse.

Her arms were tucked into the tight space, pressed awkwardly against her torso while her legs were crammed up against her ribs. I could see a dark rim of dampness on the bottom edge where the hood had been left open, allowing rain in. A shiver that had nothing to do with the dampness in the air raced down my spine and I took a step backward.

It explained why she'd not come back to relieve Sage after her break. But who would have wanted to kill her? And why put her in the boot of the car? I had the keys on me, but hadn't locked it this morning. So, at least that explained how they could have gained access. I took a shuffling step away from the car. I needed to do something. My fingers trembled again as I fished my phone from my jacket pocket.

"Call the police," I prompted myself. It took extra effort to remember to dial 9-1-1 instead of the British 9-9-9 line. That wouldn't do me much good on this side of the pond.

The line rang four or five times before someone answered on the other end. "9-1-1, what is your emergency?" a flat, feminine voice replied.

"Uh, I need the police. Someone's dead," I said, the words catching in my throat.

"Are you certain the person is dead, ma'am?"

"Yes. There's no pulse. Please, send the police. I'm in the employee lot at High Time."

"And what is your name?"

"Darcy. Darcy Ingram."

"Stay where you are, Darcy. Someone will be with you soon."

The lackluster quality of her voice didn't reassure me. I started to pace as I waited for the cavalry to appear. As far as I knew, Brookhaven's police force consisted of the Chief of Police and one officer. And the Chief was not my biggest fan. While on holiday here a few months ago, I'd solved a theft that occurred at High Time, and he'd been less than thrilled I'd stepped in on his investigation. Maybe I would get lucky and Vinnie, the young officer who'd helped on the case, would respond to my call.

A siren blared briefly in the distance before a patrol car pulled into the lot. The lights weren't flashing, and it became clear that the siren was just a show of authority. To my surprise, the sound hadn't drawn any nosy neighbors or employees. The enormity of the fact I'd discovered a dead body overwhelmed the latent curiosity that no one else had come to investigate. No one but I knew for sure that Vera was dead. My stomach dropped as the driver's side door opened and Chief Rick Hayes stepped out. His vibrant blond hair was mostly hidden behind his wide-brimmed police hat. As he straightened to his full height, I was reminded of how formidable this man had been during our last encounter.

Our gazes met and immediately his eyes narrowed in suspicion. They were an eerie shade of brown with almost amber flecks in them that reminded me of a wild animal. I stayed where I was by the open boot of Tania's car, waiting for him to make the next move.

"I see you've returned to our little haven, Miss Ingram," he said coolly.

"Liked it so much I decided to call it home," I answered.

"Is that so?"

I was surprised Ginny hadn't talked his ear off about my return. She'd had no problem doing it to anyone who would listen at the cafe. Then again, what had he told me the last time I'd relied on information from his sister? She couldn't help herself, but she wasn't always to be believed.

"You called about a dead body?" He finally said, taking a step toward me.

"I did," I responded, gesturing to Vera beside me. "I found her a few minutes ago."

He let out a sharp exhale through his nose and closed the distance between us. I had no idea if dead bodies were a common occurrence in Chief Hayes' jurisdiction, but if they weren't, his face betrayed nothing. He bent over Vera's body, studying the length of whatever was looped around her neck.

Taking a step back he pulled the radio on his belt free and spoke into it. "Vinnie, I'm going to need you to send for the coroner."

That answered my question on whether Vinnie was working. But I could have sworn that the last time I'd seen him, Vinnie had said there were other officers who worked there, too.

I didn't hear Vinnie's response over the radio, because Chief Hayes took a step back, hands on his hips. "You want to tell me how you happened upon a dead body in the trunk of another woman's car?"

My throat went dry and words failed me. Under this man's disbelieving gaze, anything I said would come out sounding like a lie. But there was nothing for me to lie about. I'd done nothing wrong. My stomach was still doing flips from whatever had made me faint, but the discomfort of being under this man's scrutiny overshadowed the belly pains. Behind Chief Hayes, the back door opened, and Thomas stuck his head out, taking in the situation. He disappeared and a moment later Sage reappeared.

"What's going on, Chief?" she called.

"Police business, Sage. Go back inside."

"It's Vera," I said before I could stop myself.

"That girl's my employee, so if something's going on with her, I deserve to know." Sage planted herself a foot from the car, hands on her hips.

Chief Hayes's shoulders slackened just a little as he pivoted to look at my boss. "It appears your employee is dead. I'm sorry. Now please, go back inside and let me get to work. And make sure no one on shift leaves until Vinnie or I have had a chance to talk to them."

The way Sage balled her hands into tighter fists against her waist and bit her lip suggested she wanted to argue, but was forcing herself to comply with his instructions. My heart hurt for her. In only a few months, two crimes had befallen her establishment. It couldn't have happened to a nicer person.

Chief Hayes turned back to face me. "Since you found the victim, I'll need you to come down to the station and give a statement."

I nodded mutely just as a dark windowless van with the word Coroner emblazoned on the side pulled into the parking lot. A second squad car pulled up right behind it and Vinnie climbed out. He wore a hat similar to Chief Hayes' and I spotted the word Deputy on the badge pinned to his chest.

So that was why the chief had called Vinnie directly. He'd landed himself a promotion since the last time I'd been in town.

"Miss Ingram, welcome back," Vinnie said with a genuine smile.

"Thanks," I managed before Chief Hayes spun to face his deputy.

"We've got a dead employee by the name of Vera. I need you to start taking witness statements inside. Find out what they were doing in the last three to four hours."

"You got it, Chief," Vinnie said with a salute before following Sage back inside the building.

That left me standing alone once again with Chief Hayes. I'd found Vera's body and that raised questions. I still owed him an explanation about why I was out here in the first place. He had to know this wasn't my car.

I climbed into the back of his cruiser and watched as the coroner lifted Vera's body out of the car and onto a gurney. Chief Hayes climbed behind the wheel, maneuvering around the other cars with ease. It was a short trip from High Time along Main Street to the police station.

Despite the emptiness of the station, I couldn't shake the feeling of someone's gaze watching me. I wrapped my arms around my torso to ward off the sense of unease as Chief Hayes led me through a door to a short hallway with harsh cinder block walls. A door at the far end opened into a room with a single window. Maybe I'd watched too many cop shows, but I doubted I'd see anyone observing through the window once inside.

"This isn't where I gave my statement last time," I noted, hovering on the opposite side of the table as Chief Hayes sat down.

"Fender benders and dead bodies aren't the same thing, Miss Ingram. Now, sit down."

He could have said please.

I perched on the edge of the seat and laid my hands flat on the table. He studied me in silence for a long minute. Probably to see if I squirmed. Finally, he pulled out a notepad and pen from his shirt pocket.

"So, why don't you tell me how you came to find that young woman's body."

"I was heading home. Well, to the bed and breakfast. I'm boarding there," I rambled.

"Going home in the middle of a workday?" he interrupted.

"I wasn't feeling well. I don't think my lunchtime coffee agreed with me. Queasy stomach, nausea. I was about to get in the car when I got sick in the bin behind the shop."

"What prompted you to go to the trunk? I'm pretty sure most people don't keep antacids there."

"We'd borrowed the umbrella in the morning, and I was putting it in the backseat when I saw the boot was open. I assumed Vera had left it open when she got the umbrella this morning. I was worried about water from the storm getting into the compartment, so I went to check. That's when I found her."

"And you said her name was Vera?"

"Yes. She came to stay at Tania's about a week ago. Got a job working the front counter at High Time."

"So, you carpooled today, then?"

"Yes."

"And you borrowed Tania's car?"

"Yeah. She said she didn't need it today and given the rain, we didn't want to walk," I answered.

"Any tension between the two of you?"

My mind flashed to her reaction to seeing me work actual magic on the seedling. Just because Tania knew about my magic didn't mean the whole town had to. Then again, I'd sort of confessed my magic to Chief Hayes when I helped solve the robbery at the dispensary. Another image popped into my mind's eye—whatever had been looped around Vera's throat. It could have been a plant or a vine of some sort. If I admitted Vera had seen me using plant magic, that would look like I had a reason to kill her. But if I left it out completely and someone else had overheard, my omission would appear even worse.

"Not really. I guess we had a little disagreement this morning about how I was tending the plants, but it didn't seem like a big deal. Like I said, she worked the front counter, so she didn't really have experience with how I handle the plants." I took a breath. "We didn't know each other all that well. She was quiet. Kept to herself most of the time. Although, I did overhear her arguing with a customer right before lunch."

"What were they arguing about?" He sat; pen poised over his pad.

"I don't know. But I heard him call her a different name." I rubbed at my temples. My stomach was threatening a second revolt against my midday meal and I doubted if the chief would appreciate it. "Kenna or something like that. I was in another room, but she seemed pretty upset. I tried to offer her some moral support, but she said she wanted to be alone."

"Did you get a look at this customer?"

"No. He was gone by the time I got to the front of the store."

"But you're certain it was a man? Even though, as you just said, you didn't see him?" he probed.

"I know what a man's voice sounds like, Chief," I retorted.

"You only recently came to Brookhaven, is that correct?"

"It is. Sage sponsored my visa and I got lucky that it was approved so quickly."

He made a noncommittal noise and glanced at his notepad. "Tell me, Miss Ingram, am I going to find your fingerprints on the body?"

My throat turned to sandpaper, I couldn't swallow and I couldn't breathe. "What?" the word barely squeaked out.

"Am I going to find your fingerprints on the victim's body?"

"I don't ... I mean I checked for a pulse," I stammered.

"Can you tell me what you were doing before you found the body?" he pressed. "Before the part about getting sick in the trash."

I wanted to wipe the sweat from my palms, but that would make me look guilty. And I hadn't done anything wrong. I knew I hadn't. "I went for lunch at Ginny's. Then when I got back I wasn't feeling well."

'What time did you leave and return?"

"I left around noon. Maybe a little after. I ate a quick sandwich and got my coffee to go after I finished my meal. Then, I got back to the shop and …"

"And?" He prodded.

"I think I must have blacked out for a bit. Because I remember waking up on the floor in the grow room, coffee all over the floor. And it was after two o'clock. I'd gotten back around one."

"So, you have an hour unaccounted for. Did anyone see you?"

"No. Only Sage comes in, but I think she was still at the front. Vera took an early lunch after the argument with that customer. And I guess she never came back."

Chief Hayes didn't respond. But the intensity of his gaze warned that he didn't like what he was hearing. And truth be told, neither did I. Someone had killed Vera, likely between the time I saw her last and when I came to. *Had I been the last person to see her alive?* The way Chief Hayes watched me, like he was stalking prey suggested something far worse. He thought I'd done something to her.

"I think I have everything I need for now," Chief Hayes said, pulling me from my musings. "This goes without saying, Miss Ingram, but don't leave town."

"Am I free to go?" It came out as a whisper.

"For now. But I'm sure we'll be seeing a lot of each other."

I did my best not to run out of the interrogation room screaming. I managed a respectable power walk to the front of the station where I found Tania waiting. She gave me a look that was part frustration and part amusement.

"You must really have it out for my car."

5

J stared at Tania in stunned silence for a minute, my mind trying to parse out her meaning. It got derailed by a more pressing question that short-circuited the rest of my body. *How did she know I was here?* As far as I'd known, she had plans to stay in all day, because of the weather. But, the rain had let up. Maybe she'd gone out for a walk. She had every right to do so. Then again, small towns bred gossip, especially if people were being questioned by the police at High Time. It's possible someone had already shared the news of Vera's death. And why did Tania sound so cheery?

"My apologies. That was in poor taste," Tania said after I'd stared at her blankly for what seemed an eternity. "Come along. Let's go home."

I trailed after the older woman, feeling like I'd been sent home from the headmaster's office in school, being collected by a disapproving parent. I finally fell into step beside her as we passed Ginny's.

"How did you know I was at the station?" The words finally dislodged themselves from my throat.

"I was on Main Street when the police cars and the coroner's van went by. I saw you get in Chief Hayes' car. It wasn't hard to figure out where you'd gone after that."

"Vera's dead," I blurted. A part of me hadn't fully processed the fact that I'd found a young woman's body in my landlady's car.

"You're sure it was her?" Tania pressed.

"I ... found her," I murmured and leaned in close. "And I think Chief Hayes thinks I had something to do with it."

The gentle hand she placed on my shoulder was enough to dissolve the barrier keeping my emotions in check. Until now, I'd felt numb, cut off from what I'd witnessed. But now, it came welling up within me, threatening to drown me in sorrow. I hadn't known Vera well, but the loss of her life still hurt. I bent double; hands pressed to my knees as I tried to catch my breath. Air came in ragged gasps and all the while Tania kept a hold on me. Just enough to reassure me I wasn't alone.

"Why don't we get you somewhere where you can sit down," Tania said and guided me inside the café.

We took a booth at the back, as far from the prying eyes of the other patrons—namely Ginny—as possible. News of Vera's death had already reached the tiny café. I heard people whispering about a woman's body being found at High Time. One man who sat at the end of the counter closest to us set down his glass and addressed no one in particular, "If you ask me, that place is cursed."

Tania had remained quiet until our server had come and gone, taking our drink orders. I pulled a napkin free of the dispenser on the table and dabbed at my cheeks.

"Now, tell me why you believe Rick thinks you did this," Tania prompted softly.

"I was the one who found the body. I can't account for where I was when she was killed," I answered.

"You were at work, weren't you?"

My stomach rumbled, reminding me that I'd been on the way home to rest. "Something I ate or drank earlier didn't agree with me. Made me really nauseous. Then I think I passed out. When I came to, it was nearly an hour later."

"That's strange. And no one came to check on you?"

"No. I woke up alone in the grow room. I suppose none of the staff in the kitchen had a reason to come looking. They had all they needed for the day's preparations. And Sage was busy at the front covering for Vera."

Tania sipped from her cup of coffee, contemplating my words. As her dark gaze bore into my own, I couldn't help feeling like she was trying to gauge my emotions. Best of luck to her. I wasn't sure I could sort through them all myself. I didn't envy her trying to sort them out.

Finally, she said, "We're going to figure out what happened. The good news is Rick hasn't charged you with anything yet."

"Can you believe that poor girl, murdered?" Ginny's voice carried across the space. "It's almost like someone didn't like her being the newest face in town."

I bristled as her voice faded and more gazes turned toward me. I wasn't prone to hating people, but Ginny was doing a good job at testing my limits.

Across the booth from me, Tania turned her head and glared in Ginny's direction.

"She can't be serious," I huffed, slinking down in the seat.

"Don't let her bother you. She's just bored and gossiping keeps her the center of attention," Tania answered.

"She can't really think I've done anything, can she? I'd never want to hurt anyone. I mean, sure I got a little upset Vera lashed out this morning when she walked in on me trying to use magic. But that didn't mean I'd want to kill her for it. And even if I wanted to, I am not capable of that," I protested, as if making my case to my landlady would make all the difference in the world. She wasn't the person I had to convince.

"Oh, I'm sure she doesn't. See, for Ginny, she doesn't have to be right. People just have to think there's a chance that she knows something, because of her connection with Rick and the family name. I'm surprised she hasn't told you yet, but their family dates all the way back to the Witch Trials."

"She's a witch, too?" I rasped.

"I told you this was a safe place to practice magic. You didn't think that was just because I was here, did you? This place attracts the supernatural."

"Anyway, if something Ginny says turns out wrong, well then someone else lied, not her."

"Must be nice to be so privileged," I grumbled.

Tania sighed. "I can understand your frustration. And believe me, even if I weren't an empath, I'd be feeling it from here. But being mad at Ginny for doing what's in her nature isn't going to get you anywhere."

"So, what am I supposed to do?"

"Find out what really happened to Vera," Tania pointed out as if it were the most obvious thing in the world.

"You're joking. Remember what happened last time I looked into a crime?"

"Yes, you caught a thief and landed yourself a respectable job," she replied with a smirk.

"And I pissed off the town's law enforcement and made people suspicious of me."

"Well, not everyone is going to like you, Darcy. But that shouldn't matter. If you think that this investigation is going to try and pin this crime on you, then you have every right to find out the truth to protect yourself."

"I just wish I knew more about Vera. I told Chief Hayes about the customer she argued with this morning, but he didn't seem to believe me. And I'm sure Sage would turn over any video footage that was available. I know she's got cameras."

"What customer?" The clipped way Tania spoke suggested she had more to say, but kept quiet.

"I didn't really see them, but it was a man's voice. He called her the wrong name and that seemed to upset her. That's when I stepped in. I tried to be supportive, but she'd seen me using magic earlier and was angry I'd tried to convince her she hadn't seen it."

"What were you doing?"

"Trying to get a plant to grow. And I was having a little success until she interrupted me."

"I know it probably doesn't seem like it, but that's good progress."

"Thanks. Too bad all I'm going to remember from today was finding a dead body in your car," I murmured.

I didn't like being somewhere so public. Not when Ginny's mouth was turning people's suspicions my way one syllable at a time. My stomach had settled a touch now, too.

"I want to find out what happened. You're right that I need to know if I'm going to make sure I don't get blamed, but there's little else we can do here. If we're going to find anything else out about Vera or who might want to hurt her, it's going to be at the B&B."

"You aren't wrong," Tania agreed, but didn't move.

I heard the tinkle of the tiny bell above the entrance as the door opened. A man walked in, scanning the space for an available seat. Finally, he settled on one of the empty stools at the counter at the far end of the room. It wasn't the bearded man from the day Vera arrived, but I didn't think I'd seen this man before either. I tracked our server heading over with a half-full coffee pot. She stopped for longer than necessary to fill his cup, flashing a flirty smile his way before Tania flagged her down.

"You sure you don't want anything to eat?" the server asked with a pout.

"We're sure, Nancy. Just stopped in for a quick coffee," Tania answered and laid a couple of bills on the table.

Nancy gave me a side eye as I followed Tania out of the cafe and up Main Street toward the B&B. It felt strange to be making the short trek without a car, even though I'd been getting to High Time by foot since I'd started there. I paused, momentarily forgetting Sage had given me her blessing to go home for the rest of the day.

"I really am sorry about your car. It's probably going to be impounded again," I blurted as we reached the front porch of the house.

"I told you, I was only joking earlier. Though I am wondering if someone decided to put a curse on the car. There was that funny bit about the title when I bought it ..." she trailed off, falling into Spanish.

My landlady was full of stories I could only hope to one day unravel about her experience with different types of magic. Now was not the time to probe about her potentially cursed car. The sense of dread that had clung to me like a wet blanket since calling 9-1-1 still hung heavy as I stepped into the foyer. I'd hoped being back on familiar ground would ease some of the apprehension, but if anything, the familiarity made it heavier, pressing against my chest and making it difficult to catch my breath. Sadness ebbed, replaced by anger, and then fear cascaded over me, turning my insides to ice.

Is this what grief feels like?

"Don't let everything overwhelm you. Focus on one emotion and let that fill you up," Tania called from the kitchen.

I guess empaths are good for more than just sussing out criminal motives. After all, it was her power that had told us the thief that had rear-ended us on my first trip to town had been confident of their escape. I liked to think that was part of what helped lead me to the identity of the thief.

I did my best to do as Tania had suggested and focused on the anger bubbling in my chest. I let it burn hot and fierce within me, hardening into resolve to find out what had happened to Vera.

"Careful, my dear. Anger is a powerful emotion, but it can easily blind you," Tania warned, returning to the foyer.

"I'm fine," I answered, starting up the stairs to the bedrooms.

Patience, a disembodied voice echoed in my head.

I hadn't seen Beau lurking until I put my hand on the banister and instead of smooth wood, my fingertips met scaly skin. The chameleon's body rippled, discarding the browns of the wood, and taking on his normal greenish color. I wasn't in the mood to be lectured by a telepathic herbivore. He blinked up at me expectantly. Like he wanted me to acknowledge that I'd understood his message.

"Girl, you are the talk of the town," Sam announced, materializing at the top of the staircase.

"Really? I hadn't noticed," I replied in a droll tone.

"Don't worry, I know you're not a killer," he replied, floating down a couple of steps so we were eye to eye. "Though, I bet if you were the kind of girl to take out her rivals, it wouldn't have been Vera."

No, it wouldn't.

A shiver danced down my spine. I hated having such dark thoughts. I wasn't a violent person. I could never hurt someone, not even Ginny. No matter how much I'd love to stop her gossiping.

"Behave yourself, Sam," Tania called up the stairs.

"I'm only saying what I see, Tia," he answered with a shrug of one sequined shoulder.

As he descended the staircase without his feet touching the steps, I pondered how he was able to change outfits so frequently. They were always outlandish. I'd seen him in no less than five or six outfits since I'd been here. I'd tried to ask him, but he'd flat out ignored me.

A mystery for another day.

"If you're so in the know about what's happening around town, what's your theory?" I called after him, pivoting on the stairs and starting back to the ground level.

"What do I look like, a detective?" he replied dismissively.

That was less than helpful. What was the point of having a ghost who could flit around town unseen if he wasn't going to be useful? I cast a glance over to the banister at Beau. Our gazes met and he disappeared into the varnished wood surface again. I hadn't heeded his words and now he was ignoring me, too. I'd have to do the digging on my own. I knew Tania would offer her assistance, but she'd already been dragged into too much drama and misfortune by her proximity to me two months ago. I could spare her the frustration of having to prove my innocence. Besides, I could do this on my own. I was a strong, capable woman with magic that sometimes did what I wanted. I could solve a murder.

I was halfway up the stairs again when someone pounded on the front door. I froze in place, waiting for Tania to answer it. Time slowed as I watched my host approach the door. The look on her face fell somewhere between irritation and resignation. I couldn't say whose emotions she channeled in that moment.

"I do hope you've come to tell me you can return my property," she said to the person on the other side of the door. I couldn't make out faces.

"Afraid not, Tia," Chief Hayes answered.

I heard the crinkling of paper passing from one

hand to the other. "We've got a warrant to take Ms. Chase's belongings and search for any other evidence that may be linked to her murder. I'm afraid while we do that, we're going to need you to temporarily vacate the premises."

"You can't be serious," she protested, temper accentuating the Spanish lilt of her voice.

"We'll be done as quickly as we can. A few hours at most," Vinnie's voice floated up the stairs to me.

I tried to make my legs move in either direction. Either way I went, they would accuse me of acting in a suspicious manner. Oh, how I wished my magic allowed me to teleport. At least that way, I could pop out in the kitchen and then I wouldn't look like I'd been rummaging through a dead woman's belongings.

Finally, I managed to go downstairs and offered as nonguilty a look as I could to the two officers hovering in the foyer. I wanted to tell Sam to pay attention to whatever the police found, but I had a feeling Sam would be haunting them every step of the way anyway. Maybe I couldn't do this whole investigating thing on my own after all.

6

$\mathcal{I}$ followed Tania out the front door and onto the porch. I thought I caught a glimpse of Sam's translucent form flutter by the upper window before Vinnie shut the door behind me.

"They can't really kick you out of your own home, can they?" I protested as we stood there.

"Seems Rick would disagree with that assessment. Not that I've any idea what they hope to find," Tania answered with a glare at the doorway before starting down the front steps. "Come on, we better not linger."

I followed her up the road toward the center of town, unsure of where we were headed. It didn't make sense to go back to Ginny's. I wasn't sure I could stand the stares and whispers Ginny's rumor mill had already generated. But there was little chance I could go back to work today, either. Everyone would know by now that I had been the one to find Vera's body.

So, where did you go in this town when the only lodging house was off limits? Tania marched onward with a confident swagger, leaving me no choice but to trail behind her. We passed by the corner where High Time sat. I half-expected Sage to have shut down for the day, but the overhead sign was lit and the small placard on the front door read 'Open.'

"How long do you think they'll keep us out of the B&B?" I called, finally falling into step beside Tania.

"As long as they think it's necessary. As frustrating as it is to be displaced, I know that Rick is going to do his very best to find out what happened to Vera. This town doesn't see much crime, but he takes his job seriously."

I'd seen his dedication in action when I'd first come to Brookhaven. He'd worked the case until he'd gotten the right man in the end, thanks to my help. I hadn't meant to insert myself in the case, but it had drawn me in. The magic that was awakening within me took hold and wouldn't let go until I'd followed the trail to the perpetrator.

"I just wish those instincts didn't make him think I did something," I grumbled.

"It is strange you don't remember what happened and that you were blacked out for over an hour," she replied, pausing at a crosswalk. She cast her gaze about, first down the length of Main Street and then up a side street called Birch.

"I have an idea," she announced and pivoted on her heel, guiding me in the opposite direction.

We ended up at a small three-story building, one of the tallest in town. It looked like the first floor had once contained a shop, but had been converted into housing. I could see someone had a TV and a lounge chair set in the front room.

"You didn't tell me there were flats for rent," I teased as Tania rang the bell from the middle unit.

"A woman's got to protect her investment," she answered with a wink.

The door to the building buzzed, letting us in. Before I could ask who we'd come to see, Tania disappeared inside. I caught the door before it could lock on me and stepped into the cool entry-way. Someone had installed a door to the left, blocking off the unit on the ground level. A narrow staircase led up to the upper floors and I could hear Tania's footfalls on the risers above me.

Hurrying to catch up, I took the stairs two at a time.

I rounded the top of the staircase just in time to see the occupant of the second floor unit open their door, revealing Maggie Henley. She served as the pharmacist at the town's clinic. She was something of a hearth witch and I'd experienced her healing salves firsthand. She, in my humble and unpracticed opinion, was a very gifted witch. She was muscular with auburn hair that she'd since styled into a close-cropped do. It came to a slight point at the front of her head. I found myself ogling her from the landing.

"I didn't know you lived here," I blurted. In all fairness, we'd only met one time at the clinic where she worked.

"Nice to see you again," she said with a grin before opening the door wider. "Although I'm kind of surprised to see you both. Is everything okay?"

"Well, the B&B is presently occupied by law enforcement and Darcy here is having some memory issues I thought you might be able to help with," Tania explained.

"Of course. Please, come in."

I didn't know what to expect when I entered her flat, but it immediately felt like it was *her*. Logically, I understood we hardly knew each other. Yet, the art pieces on the walls were a perfect reflection of her personality and powers. They were all warm hues, inviting the observer to find comfort like I knew I could in Maggie's presence.

"So why are the police at the B&B?" Maggie probed, breaking the peace that had settled around me.

"I'm sure you heard about poor Vera," Tania answered.

"Hard not to when Ginny Hayes opens her mouth," Maggie snorted before sobering and giving me a sympathetic glance. "I'm sorry you had to be the one to find Vera. How horrible."

"It was a bit of a shock," I admitted.

"And from Tania's comment earlier, it sounds like you've got some memory issues? What are you looking to recall?"

I swallowed the lump in my throat. "I can't remember anything from the time I left Ginny's at lunch and when I came into the grow room at High Time. An hour's just missing and ... Chief Hayes thinks I might have had something to do with the murder."

Maggie's cheeks flushed to within a few shades of her hair. "Most days I love that man, but sometimes he can be so infuriating. Why would he think you had anything to do with killing someone?"

I shook my head. "I guess, because I found her. It looked suspicious. But the thing is, Vera and I did sort of have a disagreement earlier and ..." I trailed off. I knew that Maggie had magic, but I had never actually told her that I did, too.

"And you're worried you might have done something and blocked it out," Maggie finished for me.

I nodded mutely. She rubbed her hands together and I expected to see them turn orange with her healing magic. "Well, I haven't used my skills for something like this, but I'll give it a try." She pointed to a door behind her. "Guest room is that way. I figure being comfortable can only help. Why don't you go have a seat and I'll be right in?"

Not wanting to delay things, I headed into the room and sat down on the bed. Like the living room, the bedroom was decorated in tasteful prints and the bedcovers were soft to the touch.

The door squeaked on its hinges, interrupting my thoughts. I turned to find Maggie standing in the doorway holding a bowl with a bluish liquid inside. Tania was nowhere to be seen.

"You have a lovely home," I said as she sat beside me.

"Thanks," she replied and settled the bowl in her lap. "It belonged to my grandmother. I moved in with her when she got sick a few years ago and she left it to me in her will when she passed. So, lucky me I don't even have to pay a mortgage."

"I'm sorry to hear about your grandmother," I said reflexively.

"It was a couple years back." She let out a sigh. "Though I will admit sometimes this place feels a little big for one person."

"So, how is this supposed to work? I'm pretty new to healing magic. Well, magic in general really," I rambled, changing subject.

"It should be a simple spell. We're going to use the infusion of periwinkle in the water to draw out any memories that might be hiding. Now, I will warn you, this might bring up more than just the memories you're looking for. It's more of a hack job than a surgical strike."

"Lucky for me I don't have any other memories hiding away," I said, a nervous laugh bubbling in my throat.

Sure, there were things I'd rather not dwell on; like my parents' rejection of my magic, but I wasn't actively trying to repress those memories. I prayed I wouldn't be accosted with visions of me strangling poor Vera for criticizing my weak attempts at plant magic. I wiped the sweat from my palms on my thighs and offered up my hands to her.

Her gentle fingers wrapped around my hands as she placed my fingers in the water. It was warm to the touch and yet it sent tiny shivers along the nerve endings in my hands. Like it was shocking them awake. The soothing scent of the periwinkle infusion tickled my nose. I could swear I heard it calling to me; urging me to use my own magic.

If only I knew how.

"I don't see anything," I said after what felt like an eternity.

"It can take time, especially if the memories are buried deep," Maggie said in a reassuring tone. Her hands tightened around me, the added pressure a reminder that she was still here with me.

We sat there, our hands dipped in the water for ages and still nothing came to the surface. Not even bad memories of my parents. That seemed odd. Was I doing something wrong? Could my magic somehow be blocking her attempts to help me remember? The last time she'd used her powers on me, it was for superficial healing. And I hadn't been using my magic as openly and frequently as I was now.

"This isn't working," I finally said, pulling my hands from the water. I held them aloft as the liquid dribbled down my fingertips and returned to the bowl with little 'plops.'

Maggie passed me a towel to dry my hands as she set the bowl on the floor between her feet. Her brow creased with frown lines as she studied her own hands. Her prolonged silence frayed my already worn nerves. She hadn't expected this to fail either.

"It's probably me," I said, trying to assuage any sense of guilt she might have about the spell not working.

"No, it's not. Well, not like you probably mean," she replied and turned to look at me. "The spell can only pull out memories that are there in the first place. It's possible you don't have any memories of that gap in time, because there weren't any to be made."

"I know I was feeling ill before I passed out, but I've never blacked out for an hour."

My stomach soured and my throat burned with acid as a realization hit me. There were ways of making someone unconscious for long periods of time. But surely no one in town would want to hurt me. *Would they?*

"I know it wasn't what you were hoping to hear,"

Maggie added, patting my forearm in an almost motherly fashion.

"I just wish I knew why all of this was happening. I mean, Vera was a nice person. She didn't deserve to die. And as selfish as it sounds, I don't deserve to be blamed for something I didn't do."

"So, do something about it," she prodded.

I'm trying.

"The last time I tried to investigate something, Chief Hayes nearly had a heart attack," I pointed out.

"Like I said, most of the time I love the man, but he is just one person and he's not infallible. He's got his blind spots just like everyone else. If you're really being blamed for this girl's death, then you better fight like hell to prove you didn't do it. Because the law might say you're innocent until proven guilty, but small towns like this operate on a guilty until proven otherwise mentality." The frustration in her voice dropped her tone a few notes into a low alto.

At least I knew I had two people in my corner. It seemed even though we'd spent very little time together, Maggie believed in me and had my back. And Tania had been the guiding force in bringing me back to Brookhaven. She'd offered me a roof over my head and given me the mentor I'd so desperately needed to understand my craft.

Before either of us could say anything more, the sound of voices drew my attention back to the living room. Tania was speaking with someone, but that didn't make sense. She wouldn't just let someone into Maggie's home. Maggie stood, artfully stepping around the bowl on the floor and pulled open the bedroom door. I was on my feet following her in seconds.

I nearly ran into Maggie as she stood in the doorway between the rooms. Sam hovered a few inches off the ground, looking more solid than I'd ever seen him. He wore what appeared to be a sequined jacket and tight leather pants. There were bits of sparkle and a rhinestone adorning his left eye.

"I thought we had an understanding," Maggie said, eying the dead man.

He gave an exaggerated eye roll. "I remember. I can't just pop in whenever I please. Something about boundaries and manners." He waved a hand dismissively.

"You ... know him?" I rasped, stepping around Maggie and into the living room proper.

"You didn't think he just kept to the B&B did you?" she snorted.

"Well, no. But I didn't realize other people could see him," I answered as embarrassment crept up my neck.

"Oh honey, you are so in need of Magic 101," Sam sighed.

He wasn't wrong. I would love for someone to sit me down and teach me all the basics, but it would have to wait until I wasn't a murder suspect. Tania cleared her throat, drawing the attention away from Sam.

"You said you had something interesting to share."

"Well, while Chief Hunky and Deputy Ditzy were snooping around, they found a wallet hidden under the mattress." He leaned in for dramatic effect. "It had her picture on it, but a different name."

"What was it?" I took a step closer, trying to recall the name I'd heard the customer call Vera earlier today. It, like the missing hour, seemed to have fled my mind entirely.

"Not even I can read through pockets," Sam retorted. "They wrapped that baby up real quick when they uncovered it."

"Is that all they found?" Tania pressed.

Sam shrugged one shiny shoulder. "I figured that was the more interesting bit of their investigating," he replied, raising his hands to put air quotes around the last word.

Being in possession of a fake ID certainly seemed suspicious, but it didn't usually lead to murder. There was more to the story that we didn't know. I'd hoped Sam's arrival would shed some light on Vera's death and at least give us a motive, not leave me with more questions.

7

Maggie had insisted we stay for dinner. By the time we'd finished, it was late enough she'd then told us to stay the night. Sleep had eluded me though, despite the comfortable bed and the soothing cup of tea from Maggie that I was almost certain carried some hint of magic in it. I tossed and turned, seeing Vera's blank gaze staring up at me every time I shut my eyes. By six in the morning, I'd given up trying and crept into the living room and the attached kitchen, rooting around for some coffee.

"Couldn't sleep?" Maggie's voice carried from the couch.

I turned, coffee filter in hand, to find her sitting up. She'd insisted Tania and I each take the bedrooms. Her hair was mussed from the pillow, but it only served to accentuate her wide eyes and the roundness of her cheeks. "I tried. Just couldn't manage it," I answered.

"I'm not surprised. It's not every day you find a dead body. If you'd slept soundly, I'd be worried." She pushed the blankets off and came to join me in the kitchen.

"I kept thinking about what Sam said, that they found an ID with a different name," I said, my hands working on autopilot to fill the pot with water. Maggie gestured to a container of coffee beans beside the machine, and I poured them in. "There was a man she was arguing with before we both went on break and he called her a different name. But for the life of me I can't recall what it was."

"Have you told Rick about it?"

I nodded. "Not that he seemed to buy it. I mean, I didn't see the man's face, just heard his voice."

"And let me guess, it was just the two of you around when it happened?"

Another nod. "But I know Sage has cameras for anti-theft purposes. Surely Chief Hayes would look into it, right?" My voice weakened on the last word, conveying my own fear that he wouldn't follow up.

"Like I said, he's thorough. I have no doubt he'll

find out what happened." She reached around me and pulled down two ceramic mugs from over the sink just as the pot finished percolating.

Maggie snatched the pot before I could get it, filling both mugs to the brim. I thought I caught her hands shimmering orange for a split second before she handed my cup over.

"Can I ask you something?" I broached after letting the first sip fortify me.

"Anything," she replied, spinning to brace her back against the counter.

"When I first visited town, Tania mentioned something offhand about Chief Hayes not being to everyone's liking. You don't seem to mind him. What's that about?"

Maggie shook her head and clasped her mug in both hands. "When your sister is the self-appointed town gossip, it rubs some folks the wrong way to have her so close to the town's law and order. Plus, they're a legacy family and some folks don't like that they've got that much sway in town."

I could understand that. I'd fallen prey to Ginny's grapevine, and I hadn't even lived here that long. It had pushed me to accuse Sage of theft and sent Chief Hayes to her doorstep when she'd been innocent.

"Can't he rein her in?"

Maggie chuckled. "If there's one thing that has been a constant in this town since I've lived here, it's that no one tells Ginny Hayes what to do, not even her big brother."

"So, people are worried about a conflict of interest," I said, taking another long pull from my mug.

"I suppose, although I think everyone can agree that Rick Hayes has a very strong sense of justice and if Ginny landed herself on the wrong side of things, he wouldn't hesitate to bring her in."

I let her words wash over me. At least I was dealing with a law enforcement officer who wasn't going to go for the easy solution. That at least gave me a bit of a chance not to end up in jail. I let her statement hang between us in the air as we each finished our coffee. My phone beeped in my pocket, notifying me of an incoming text. Maggie set her mug in the sink and gestured wordlessly to the bathroom.

Retrieving my phone from my pocket, I found a message from Sage, asking simply, '**Can you open today? Instructions on how to set up the register are in the top drawer of my desk.**'

It wasn't what I expected, especially the day after one of her own employees was murdered. Though I sent a quick **'Sure'** back to her and retreated to the guest room to get ready. I didn't love the idea of going to work in yesterday's clothes, but they would have to do. When I emerged in my work uniform a few minutes later, I found Tania stationed at the stove.

"You aren't leaving yet, are you? You haven't even had breakfast," she called, waving a spatula in my direction.

"Sage needs me to open the shop today," I called. "I'll grab something on the way."

She made a tsking sound with her tongue to signal her disapproval that I was turning down a home cooked breakfast. I lingered at the front door long enough to see she was making stuffed French toast, the scent of vanilla and blackberries tickling my nostrils.

"I suppose it won't hurt to have a quick bite here," I relented and went in search of utensils. She didn't give me time to question how she knew where all of the ingredients were in Maggie's kitchen before setting a plate in front of me.

"Are you sure your magic doesn't extend to cooking?" I asked around a syrupy mouthful of food.

"I ask myself that every time she comes over," Maggie said, reappearing in her own work uniform.

Tania waved away the compliments and sat down at the small table. "Thank you. But really, I just inherited my mother's culinary acumen."

Our little trio sat together, enjoying the companionship. An idea began nagging me, digging itself into the back of my thoughts. If Sage was asking me to open today, that suggested she wouldn't be there for some time. Most of the other staff didn't pay me much mind. That meant if I wanted to figure out what could have motivated someone to kill Vera, I'd have time and access to check out her employment application.

It wasn't legal and could almost certainly get me sacked from my job, but it was a risk I needed to take. The only way to prove my innocence was to uncover whatever she'd been hiding. I kept my mouth shut as we finished breakfast and I started the short walk across Birch back on to Main Street.

It still amazed me that people were so trusting in small towns. Sage kept the spare key to the dispensary secreted in a fake bush at the back of the employee parking lot. She'd shown it to me not long after I'd started, insisting I know the location in case I needed to get in at odd hours to tend to the plants. There were only a couple cars in the lot as I went looking for the key. I still didn't know everyone's cars by sight. I tried the back door to find it still firmly locked though.

So, who is here already?

The metal of the key felt supercharged in my fingers as I retrieved it and headed for the back door. I couldn't stop myself from sparing a glance over my shoulder as the door handle clicked open. Holding my breath, I moved through the empty kitchen, taking note of the stations that had been prepped the night before. Cookie dough sat rising under thin films of plastic wrap and trays of gelatin were chilling in the fridge with its glass doors.

I took a cursory exam of the grow room, feeling as though I ought to check on the plants properly before I did my snooping. The tiny seedling that had been responding to my magic the day before had retreated into its potting soil. I pressed my hand to the pot, waiting to hear its soft whispers.

Silence.

"You aren't happy with me either," I sighed before checking the front of the shop. It, too, was empty, leaving just the employee break room and Sage's office.

Part of me wanted to head straight for the office and Vera's employee file, but I couldn't shake the feeling that I wasn't alone here. There had to be a reason for the car in the lot. I moved into the break room, the small space cast in shadows and stopped. There was a decidedly person-shaped lump in the center of the room and for a split second, my mind overlaid Vera's prone form on whomever was lying on the floor. The vision faded as quickly as it had come, replaced by a new fear. Someone else was dead.

No, it can't be another body.

My right hand groped along the wall until I found the light switch, flicking it to the on position. The sudden burst of light blinded me and the figure sprawled on the floor between the benches. I blinked spots out of my eyes to find Thomas laid out on a portable camp bed under a thin blanket, his dark dreadlocks flung over half of his face. He sat upright, looked around dazedly at me and nearly tumbled the short distance to the ground.

"What are you doing here?" he said, scurrying to find his footing.

"I could ask you the same," I replied. "Sage asked me to open the shop today," I added.

"Oh." He looked around the break room and then back to me. "Can we, uh, keep this between us?"

"Mind telling me why you're sleeping in the break room overnight?" I probed.

"I'd rather not," he answered, rubbing at his neck in the universal sign of embarrassment.

"I'm pretty sure even Sage would frown on you sleeping here," I noted.

Thomas bent and gathered up the blanket and pillow, folding them up before storing them in his locker. He set about collapsing the camp bed and stowing it in the utility closet on the opposite wall.

"I had a fight with my roommate and he kicked me out. It won't last. He always comes around in the end, but this is somewhere I know I'm welcome. Please, don't tell Sage."

I felt for him and sleeping here was better than on the street. "I'll make you a deal. You work out your drama with your roommate by week's end and I won't say a word to Sage," I offered.

"Thanks." He retreated to his locker to grab a clean shirt and some toiletries.

I waited for him to disappear into the bathroom before making my way into Sage's office. There was every chance Thomas would find me snooping, but I could always tell him it was on Sage's direction. After all, I needed to get the till ready out front and she kept the money in the safe behind her desk.

"Think Darcy," I said, forcing myself to take slow, steady breaths as I stood in the center of the room.

I knew that Vera had filled out a paper application. It's all Sage took, so it shouldn't be that difficult to find it. I started with the drawers of the faux wood desk, but only found folders labeled for receipts and tax records. I spun in the chair and spotted a stout two-drawer filing cabinet in the corner with a tiny gold key protruding from the topmost drawer. I turned it, pulling my sleeve down to cover my fingertips and found a handful of slim manilla folders labeled with employee names. I spotted Vera's at the back—thank you alphabetization—and pulled it out. The folder contained a photocopy of her ID listing her as Vera Chase along with the paper application. Nothing else in the way of identification filled the file.

Her handwriting was almost as terrible as mine. Her letters squished together to become nearly illegible. I skimmed through, flipping to the last page where she'd written down two references. I had no way to know if Sage had called them or not. I thought I spotted some smudge marks next to one of the names that could have been a check mark, but it could have always just been a plain old smudge. It was a risk I would have to take.

Reaching out to her references might give me a clue as to why someone would want her dead. Besides, it might explain why she had an ID with another name on it. Not wanting to risk Sage seeing the phone calls on the company phone log, I snapped a photo of the last page and retreated to the grow room where I knew I wouldn't be disturbed for at least ten minutes until whoever Sage had called in to man the till showed up. I hadn't seen Thomas emerge from the bathroom yet, but I assumed he'd be heading straight to the kitchen to start his own work for the day.

The air was damp with the artificial temperature controls keeping the plants happy and it left an uncomfortable residue on my skin. Tiny goose-bumps popped up along my forearms that I couldn't entirely attribute to the temperature. My instincts screamed at me not to do this. I pushed those fears down as I triple checked the number for the second reference before hitting the 'Call' button. I paced, waiting as the line rang three times. Four times. Five times.

I was about ready to give up, assuming it was too early for anyone to be working when a raspy female voice answered, "Hello?"

I fumbled the phone in surprise that my call had

been answered. "Uh, good morning. Is this ... Miss Hampton," I said, hurriedly flipping back to the picture I'd taken to see what name Vera had listed.

"Yeah, who is this?" Her voice carried the tone of a heavy smoker.

"My name is Sage," I lied. "I'm calling for a reference check on a former employee of yours."

"That so?" Her voice dripped with sarcasm and irritation. "Who are you looking for?"

"Vera Chase. She put in an application as a Sales Associate with us and we're just doing our due diligence to check her out. Make sure she's a good worker," I explained. It was easier to stick to a version of the truth. This woman didn't need to know Vera was working at a pot dispensary. For all I knew, Miss Hampton wasn't a fan of marijuana.

"Look, Saffron was it?" She didn't give me a chance to correct her on my false identity. "I don't know anyone by that name and I don't appreciate being pranked. Don't call here again."

She ended the call before I could respond. I tried the second number, but it went straight to voicemail. I didn't leave a message. I sank into the metal chair by the seedling's pot and stashed my phone in my pocket.

Why would Vera put down references for people

who didn't know her? Had she just guessed at the names and numbers? Or had she given them false information, too?

"Who are you, Vera?" I whispered to the plants. Not surprising, they didn't respond.

I had to hope the rest of the day would be more illuminating than the morning. Otherwise, I could be sitting behind bars by lunch.

8

Trying to act like nothing was out of the ordinary proved more than I could take. Even though I sequestered myself in the grow room for the morning, by lunch, I could hear the whispers whipping around the kitchen. The bakers kept giving me furtive glances whenever I walked through.

"I can't believe she's in today," one of them said in a stage whisper as I walked by on my way out to find some lunch.

Keep it together, Darcy.

I spun on my heel to offer up a retort when Sage stuck her head out of the office. "I know that we are all dealing with grief and shock from losing one of our own in different ways, but I will not have any of you making accusations without all the facts."

"Besides, I thought people were supposed to be innocent until proven guilty in this country." The words flew past my lips before I could think better of them.

Maggie's words about the court of public opinion rang in my ears. Even if I could prove to Chief Hayes I wasn't a killer, I'd still have to find a way to salvage my reputation with the rest of the town. I could see their vantage point in a sense. I was new to town and things had been safe before I showed up.

I left the kitchen behind and headed to the break room. Sage appeared behind me as I prepared to clock out. "Heading for lunch?"

"Yeah, if that's okay?" I answered.

"Sure. And just so you know, after today we're going to be operating on shortened hours. Ten o'clock to two o'clock."

"Because of Vera?"

She nodded as I finished clocking out. Leaving the dispensary behind, I roamed along Main Street. My feet carried me on autopilot toward Ginny's, but I couldn't bear to sit and listen to Ginny hold court from the counter. I forced myself to take a hard left and head toward the pier.

"Darcy?" Maggie's voice floated to me on the breeze from somewhere behind me.

I stopped walking and glanced over my shoulder. Sure enough, she was standing on the other side of the street headed in the opposite direction. I darted across the road without looking. Not the smartest move, but there were so few people on the road in Brookhaven it was low risk.

"Sorry, I was kind of in my own thoughts. I didn't see you," I said.

Maggie flashed me an understanding smile. "Figured as much. I also figured you weren't likely to go to Ginny's for lunch," she said, holding up a paper bag. Something spicy wafted from it, making my stomach gurgle with hunger and my mouth water.

I tugged at a few loose curls. "I know I'm innocent. At least I'm pretty sure, but I just can't handle everyone else judging me just because I found the body."

Maggie nodded and gestured toward the pier with the bag. "Tania made empanadas and there is no way I can eat all of this on my own. How about a picnic lunch?"

"Sounds lovely," I answered and followed behind her.

I'd only been to the pier once in my time living

in Brookhaven. The major festivities had already happened for the summer season, although I spotted a few larger boats out on the water. A small wooden sign offering day cruises caught my attention long enough to satisfy the spark of curiosity within me.

We found an empty table at the end of the pier. It was far enough away from other passersby that I didn't feel like everyone was looking at me, but afforded me the vantage point of seeing who else was around us. While Maggie set out the empanadas on paper plates Tania had packed, I people watched. It wasn't nearly as busy as I had expected. Free standing stalls did periodic business and occasionally couples strolled by hand in hand. A slender figure caught my attention halfway down the pier. A man paced back and forth as if he was unsure which way to go. The memory of a man walking into Ginny's a week ago flashed through my head. Could it have been the same man?

"Do you know that guy?" I asked Maggie, gesturing over my shoulder.

She glanced the way I'd pointed, and her brows knit together. "Don't think so. And I know pretty much everyone in town."

He turned my way and I ducked my gaze. After a few more turns, he disappeared.

Weird.

Maggie's sigh of exasperation was enough to draw me back to the food. I looked down and tried to figure out what had frustrated her. The empanadas smelled heavenly and my mouth literally watered at the scent.

"Utensils," Maggie announced unceremoniously, leaving me at the table to go in search of forks and knives.

I picked at one corner of the food on my plate, pulling enough of it free to get a taste. *Mmm.* I didn't care what Tania said, her food was absolutely magic. The tiny hairs on the nape of my neck bristled as I felt the intensity of someone's gaze on me. I peered over my right shoulder, but nothing obvious stood out. When I turned back to the table, Beau sat curled up by my plate.

In my hurry to leave yesterday, I hadn't even thought about him staying behind. Chameleons, magical or not, were delicate creatures and needed a lot of care. At least that's what my internet research had told me. Had he hitched a ride with Tania, and I just hadn't realized it?

"Sorry I forgot about you," I whispered.

Beau blinked up at me. I expected to hear his little voice in my head, but he remained silent. *Great, now I've got a magical creature mad at me.* Patching things up with Beau would just have to go on my increasing list of things to do once I made sure I didn't wind up behind bars. Along with learning to control my magic.

Maggie returned and sat down, handing me a plastic set of utensils. She glanced once at Beau before digging into her food. Maybe he'd hitched a ride here with her. She knew about magic, so having a telepathic reptile must not be that unusual. Beau shimmered and turned to dark brown and black hues to match the table beneath him. I knew he was there. Yet even my brain and eyes told me there was a blank table beside me.

"I wish Sam had paid more attention to what the ID said. Knowing she had a fake ID is one thing, but that doesn't help us figure out why someone would want her dead," I sighed.

"Her identity wasn't the only thing she was hiding," Maggie said off-handedly.

"What?"

Maggie averted her gaze as I waited for her to explain herself. "When she first got to town, she stopped by the clinic looking for some ointment to put on some bruises. It looked like someone might have been hurting her."

Escaping an abusive relationship would certainly explain both why she might have a fake ID on her and why someone might come looking to do her harm.

"Did you tell anyone?"

"I didn't think much of it until this morning. And honestly, I feel like I'm no better than Ginny, sharing other people's private business."

"You should tell Chief Hayes."

"That I gave her a treatment a week ago and that she didn't tell me anything about where the bruises came from?" She leaned over the table. "Besides, the bruises would have been gone by now. I do very good work and they were already healing when she came to me."

"But it would point to someone else being involved. Especially if the bruises were older than when she got here," I urged.

Maggie looked me straight in the eye. "I try not to get involved in police affairs. But I'll speak to Rick," she said softly.

There was hope for me yet. "I keep thinking about how I left things with Vera," I sighed.

"What do you mean?" Maggie propped her elbows on the table and leaned forward.

"She saw me trying to do magic. I lied to her and said she didn't see what she thought she saw. She wasn't too happy about that. Then there was her argument with the customer and she left. I hate to think I could have done something to save her if I was in fact the last person to see her before she was killed."

Maggie set her fork down. "You weren't," she said.

Plastic cutlery fell from my fingers to the table with a rattle. "What?"

"Here I go gossiping again ..." she mumbled to herself before continuing. "I was on my lunch break. I'd come outside for a little air since it had finally stopped raining and I saw Vera leave High Time."

I craned my neck back toward Main Street. I hadn't totally memorized the town's layout yet, but I didn't think you could see the entrances and exits of the dispensary from the clinic.

"In case it wasn't obvious, I like to walk," Maggie added. "Anyway, she looked upset. I was going to go over and see if she was okay, but there was no need."

"Why not?" The empanada in my belly grew cold with worry.

"Because Tania spotted her and got to her first. I didn't see where they went, but I know they went off together somewhere."

"You mean Tania was the last person to see her alive, not me? And you didn't think that was important to tell anyone?" I railed.

"It wasn't my business. And I assumed she would have already talked to Rick about it. She's not shy about speaking up."

"Well, she hasn't said a word to anyone. Don't you think that's suspicious?"

"If she hasn't said anything, I'm sure she has a reason," Maggie replied, pushing the remnants of her lunch around the plate.

Part of me felt selfish for expecting these people who barely knew me to stick their necks out for me. They had their own lives, and they weren't required to do anything for me. But they had also taken me in and promised to guide me on this magical journey. I couldn't help feeling a little betrayed.

I turned my attention to the spot where Beau had last been. I gently nudged the space with the back of my hand to confirm he hadn't made a stealth exit before addressing the creature.

"Do you have anything to say on the matter?"

'More secrets.'

"Not helpful," I snapped and stood up. Maggie didn't react to my outburst. The day had started out on a hopeful note. I'd thought maybe I could unravel this mystery, but the more time that ticked by, the less confident I was becoming. The people who were supposed to have my back were staying mum and I couldn't figure out why.

"Thanks for lunch," I said, tossing my half-eaten empanada in a nearby trash bin and beginning the trek back to the dispensary. I heard the scrape of Maggie's seat pushing away from the table, but I kept walking. If she wouldn't tell Chief Hayes about Tania, then I would. Not that I relished being in the man's presence again. There was something almost predatory about the way he looked at me when he'd brought me in for questioning.

I made it halfway to High Time when my phone rang in my pocket. I didn't recognize the number flashing on the screen as I answered.

"Hello?"

"Miss Ingram?" Vinnie's voice came over the line.

"Yes. Can I help you Deputy?"

"Chief needs you down at the station right away."

"Can I ask why?"

"Just a few more questions."

"I'm on shift," I offered lamely.

"He's already spoken to Sage."

Chief Hayes meant business. I didn't appreciate him intervening in my professional life, but maybe it was fortuitous that he needed to speak to me. He was looking for information and I had some to give. I ended the call and started back the way I'd come when I felt a pressure on my shoulder. I looked down to see Beau wrap his tail around my neck, nestle his head into the crook of my collarbone, and meld into the fabric of my brightly colored High Time shirt.

9

The sense of purpose that carried me down Main Street and to the police station evaporated the moment I stepped through the doors. Vinnie sat at his desk, gazing intently at something on his computer screen. His fingers darted over the keyboard and the screen dissolved into a lock screen bearing the town's seal the moment I approached him.

My reputation precedes me.

Although, could it really be considered a reputation if it had only happened once before? Vinnie stood and waved me onward. "He's waiting for you."

I silently wished that sentence had ended "in his office." Then, at least, it would be something of a cordial exchange of information rather than an interrogation. No such luck. Vinnie ushered me toward the interview room where I'd given my statement yesterday afternoon. Through the window, I saw Chief Hayes sitting in silence. I could see a manilla folder wedged between his hands and the angle of the paper suggested the folder sat on something that wasn't flat.

Vinnie rapped his knuckles on the door twice before opening it and letting me enter. I waited for the door to close before rounding the table and sitting in the seat opposite the Chief.

"You know, I don't appreciate you dictating my work hours like this," I said before thinking better of it.

"I'm sorry my murder investigation is inconvenient," he answered.

I forced myself to meet his gaze, not backing down from the intensity in his brown eyes. I couldn't show him that I was unnerved by the power he held over my life. "Vinnie said you had more questions for me."

"Is there anything you left out in your statement?" His voice was low.

At first, I couldn't think of anything. '*Coffee.*' Beau's voice flitted through my brain. "I told you I hadn't been feeling well and I fainted. I think it's possible someone could have drugged me."

He gave me a disbelieving glance before letting out a sigh. "Drugged how?"

"I don't know. Put something in my drink. Can't you do a blood test or something?"

"I'll see about getting someone down to do one, but even if you were, I doubt it would show up now," he said, leaving the room presumably to make that call.

I fought the urge to glance through the folder on the other side of the table in his absence. With my luck, he'd come back right as I found the good stuff. He returned a few minutes later. "Someone will be down in about twenty minutes to take a blood draw." He settled in his seat again and pressed his lips into a thin line. Waiting a beat, the chief clasped his hands in front of him and propped his elbow on the edge of the table. "You like plants."

I gawked at him. *'You like plants'* echoed in my head like a taunt. What did he know? "I suppose," I finally responded dumbly.

"Sage is very particular about the people she hires to tend to her crop, so I know that you must be very good at what you do."

Not even close.

"I think she was just grateful I helped get her money back and I was looking for a change," I answered.

He shook his head. "No, there's more to it than that. You have a way with plants."

What was he getting at? "I don't know what you're talking about," I countered. "And even if I am 'good with plants' like you say, I don't see how that's even relevant to Vera's death."

That predatory feeling I'd gotten from him before resurfaced as Chief Hayes stared at me, like he was trying to read my mind. But he couldn't do that. If he could, he'd be asking me about Tania being the last person to see Vera alive. Not grilling me about plants.

Slowly, Chief Hayes pulled the bulky item out from beneath the manilla envelope that had been concealing it. A clear evidence bag contained a coiled length the color of grass. He laid it on the table between us, lifting his gaze to meet mine.

"So, you're telling me you don't recognize this?"

I sat even straighter, and I felt Beau's tiny claws dig gently into the tender flesh near my collarbone, so he didn't fall off. The chief's accusatory tone should have made me scared, but the roiling sensation in my gut wasn't fear. It was anger and in that moment I learned it was possible to actually see red. My vision tinted at the edge and my ears pounded as blood rushed to my head. I wanted to grip the table for stability, but I knew it would only make me look guilty.

"That's right. I've no idea what that is."

"This was used to strangle Ms. Chase," he said bluntly. "Can you tell me why someone would use a length of vine to do that?"

"Because they're twisted and sick?"

I tried to study the length of the vine without reaching for it to pull it closer. I didn't recognize what it was, and it appeared to be dead by the lack of whispering in my head. Then again, I hadn't heard any of the plants at the dispensary this morning either. I'd been focused on other things, but it had become a bit of a constant low-level buzz in the back of my head. It was like white noise. But I knew that it hadn't come from the dispensary. None of the plants there had vines like this. Which meant whoever had killed Vera had come prepared and planned her murder. It hadn't been a spur of the moment act of passion.

"Where would I even have gotten hold of this?" I pressed. "Because I can tell you that it didn't come from Sage's shop. So, if you think I just grabbed the nearest thing and hurt Vera, your story is missing a few pieces."

Witnesses, I heard echo in my head.

"And anyway, if I'd left the dispensary after coming back from Ginny's, don't you think someone would have noticed?"

Like your sister.

Not that I wanted to stake my freedom on Ginny Hayes knowing everything that went on in this town. Except I suspected there was a high probability if I had gone to her shop, left, and gone out and about again, she would have noticed.

"Show me your hands," he said, shifting the conversation abruptly.

"Excuse me?" I stared in confusion at the man across the table from me. If he was trying to throw me off balance, it was working.

"Show me your hands." He repeated himself, slower this time.

I set my hands on the table for him to see. I tried not to let the subtle weight of Beau's body on my shoulder alter the way I moved. He didn't need to know I had an invisible passenger along for the ride. Although, I could do with a bit of reptilian mind reading right about now.

What's he getting at?

I felt tiny claws dig into my skin again as Beau shifted position. I suppressed the urge to shiver as his tail draped down my chest. I waited in anticipation for his little voice to pop into my head.

'Looking for evidence.'

He had to know I'd done all sorts of things since finding Vera's body, not least of which was washing my hands. There wouldn't be anything to find, even if I had been the one to kill her. Chief Hayes donned latex gloves before examining my hands, turning them palm up.

"What are you looking for?" I blurted.

'Thorns'

Beau's voice rang in my head as my gaze fell on the length of the vine sitting neatly in its little evidence bag. He was right. The vine had little prickers running its length. I hadn't noticed them when I'd discovered Vera's body in the car. Then again, I'd been more shocked to find a dead body than anything else.

"There's no proof I did anything to her," I said, letting the fact that my hands bore no wounds buoy me. "If I'd done what you said, I'd have cuts on my hands."

Chief Hayes peeled off the gloves and fixed me with an irritated glare. "Miss Ingram, this is a small town. As you might have guessed, it doesn't take long for everyone to know everyone else's business around here."

Thanks to your sister's big mouth, I thought.

"What are you implying?" I goaded.

"That it's no secret you stayed the night at Maggie Henley's apartment."

"Not just me." The words flew out of my mouth before I had even realized I'd had the thought.

"Maggie's talents are well known in town. And I would bet my badge she's got something to heal cuts."

"That wouldn't get rid of them in less than ..." I trailed off. Maggie had magic fueling her salves and ointments. It was very plausible she could create something to make my hands good as new in no time at all. She'd admitted to doing it for Vera.

"Well, she didn't," I said, my body deflating and I sank back against the hard metal chair.

"Forgive me if I don't believe you."

A knock on the door interrupted whatever he was going to say next. The door swung inward, and Vinnie appeared, escorting an older man with wire-rimmed glasses and hospital scrubs.

"You called for a blood draw, Chief?" the man said in a high tenor voice.

"I did." He showed the medic something from inside the folder as well.

"Understood." The man rounded the table. "My name is Marty. I'm going to take some blood and a cheek swab from you."

"Is the second really necessary?"

"Do you want me to note that you were being uncooperative, Miss Ingram?" Chief Hayes asked from across the table.

I shook my head and let Marty do his work. I offered up my left arm and he tied a length of latex around it, forcing my vein to the surface. I wasn't afraid of needles exactly, but I didn't need to watch as he stuck me with one.

"Open your mouth, if you would," Marty directed.

I sighed and opened my mouth, letting him swab my cheeks on both sides. It didn't thrill me that my DNA would be in the town's police database, but it was one way to definitively prove I wasn't the killer. And hopefully the blood would reveal whether I'd been drugged.

"If you don't believe me, then talk to Maggie," I said, returning to the topic of conversation. "She'll tell you that she didn't give me anything." After a beat, I added, "Am I the only person you're talking to again? Did you even ask Sage for the footage from the shop to follow up on that customer I told you about?"

"I'm following all viable leads," Chief Hayes answered as Marty finished up, pressing a tiny bit of cotton to the pinprick in the crook of my elbow. The way the chief's shoulders stiffened made him sit straighter, signaling he was offended I thought he couldn't do his job.

"Well, here's another one you ought to consider. I wasn't the last person to see Vera before she was killed. Tania Alvarez talked to her after she left High Time."

"And you conveniently omitted this fact when we spoke yesterday?"

"I didn't know it yesterday. I was talking to Maggie and she mentioned it."

Icy tendrils of guilt coiled in my belly, sending a wave of nausea cascading over me. I knew it would look bad, pointing him in Tania's direction and I was risking jeopardizing the strongest relationship I had in town. But I wasn't going to let this man, or anyone railroad me, because I was the easy target.

"I will take the information into consideration," he finally huffed before gathering the file and evidence bag.

"You know, if you want to find her killer, you should probably figure out who Vera really was," I offered.

Hayes spun on his heel and bared his teeth. "I would strongly advise you against trying to tell me how to do my job, Miss Ingram." He paused again and his lips moved like he wanted to say more.

"I know she put down fake references on her application at High Time," I said.

He arched his brow. "And how would you know that?"

"I overheard Sage checking them. The person she spoke to had never heard of Vera."

'*Liar.*'

Beau's tone was accusatory with a tinge of amusement. I needed to know what they had found in Vera's room at the B&B. What name had they found on the ID? If I could get that information, I could do a deep dive on who Vera really was.

"Am I free to go now?" I made a show of standing up anyway.

"Don't leave town," he quipped.

"Wouldn't dream of it. Especially when everyone here is so friendly," I retorted and walked out of the interview room.

I headed toward the front of the station and

expected Chief Hayes to be hot on my heels. He stopped mid-step, studying something in the file in his hands. So, I made my way past the chief's office door and spotted Vinnie sitting at his desk. He gave me a polite nod when I stopped beside him. Maybe I would get lucky and he would be sloppy, leaving evidence in plain view.

"Sorry, Chief Hayes didn't tell me if there was anything else I had to do before I left," I lied, making conversation in an effort to distract him.

"Uh, I don't think so. Just, you know, stick around."

"There's nothing keeping us from going back to the B&B right?"

"I don't make those calls, sorry, but I shouldn't think so. I know it was inconvenient yesterday," he sighed.

"You know, is it possible for me to get a copy of the statement I gave to the chief?" I blurted.

"Uh, I'll need to check the file." He gestured to the computer in front of him. "We're going digital, but it's still a work in progress."

"That would be great. Just figure I should keep hold of any legal documents with my name on them."

Glancing around the space, I noted a distinct

lack of cameras. *Good.* I waited for Vinnie to leave the room before I started rifling through the papers on his desk. Nothing of substance appeared and I was shuffling things back into place as I heard the copy machine going.

"Come on. Give me something," I muttered, easing open a drawer in the desk. It squeaked as I looked through old police reports. Finally, at the very bottom of the stack, I found a photocopy of a driver's license bearing Vera's photograph but the name McKenzie Lawson.

Gotcha.

Vinnie gave a sound of triumph and I shut the drawer, trying not to look as though I'd gone snooping in his desk. He presented me with a copy of my statement.

I cleared my throat. "Thanks. I really appreciate it."

I folded the single page into quarters and shoved it in my back pocket. I had a name to go on now. I turned to leave when the front doors whooshed open and Tania walked through. Vinnie's chair skittered back and he raced past me.

"I'm sorry to have to call you in like this," he apologized.

She waved his explanation away. "I understand,

you're just doing your job, Vinnie. I wouldn't have it any other way."

Our gazes met and I thought I caught a disapproving look before she let Vinnie lead her back toward where Chief Hayes still must have stood transfixed by his file. Clearly the chief hadn't called Tania in. Unless he'd done it and I just hadn't heard his conversation. Yet, the station wasn't that big. His voice would have carried.

'Maggie?'

For the first time all day, Beau's words came across with a hint of uncertainty. It would entirely be possible Maggie had called Vinnie like I'd begged and shared what she'd observed, leading to the call in for an interview. Whatever the reason, I was grateful the police were in fact looking at other angles. I made a mental note to ask Tania what she'd been doing with Vera or McKenzie or whatever her real name was when she'd insisted she'd be staying home all day yesterday. I should talk to Sage about the security footage. Even though Chief Hayes had said he was following all viable leads, my gut hinted he didn't think my customer was one such avenue to follow up on.

I made my way back to Main Street and looked around at the slow bustle of people going about their days. Where to go to do some digging? I wanted to avoid the coffee shop and Ginny's abnormally nosy personality. Going back to High Time would mean additional accusatory stares and whispers, and the potential for people to find me snooping.

I dialed Sage's number. It rang twice before the line picked up.

"Darcy? Are you still down at the station?"

"I've finished, but I don't think my head's in the right place to come back for the afternoon. I know it's just a few more hours, but with everything that's going on, I just need some time to clear my head. I'm sorry."

"Take the rest of today and tomorrow morning off and get your head straight. I'll pay you for sick time. You just went through something unbelievably traumatic."

Not as traumatic as being murdered.

"Thanks," I murmured.

"And being questioned by the police is never fun. I know that. Well, I guess you do, too," she added with a laugh.

My cheeks flushed. I was the reason she'd been in the exact same position I now found myself in a few months ago. "I really am sorry about all that."

"Not your fault. Anyway, seriously, take the afternoon off."

"I just feel bad leaving you down two people."

"The plants will survive a couple days without you. I promise. And I can always work the front of the store. Just because I'd prefer to be fully staffed doesn't mean I can't operate being short a couple of people." There was a brief pause on the other end of the line and I heard Sage breathing. "Some of the staff were thinking of having a little gathering on Saturday for Vera. Nothing elaborate, just some chairs out on the pier and a chance for people to share their thoughts."

"That sounds like a nice idea. I'll try to come." A gathering would be a good way to observe other potential suspects. "What if you opened it up to everyone in town? I'm sure other people would like to come and show their support."

It seemed like something a small town like Brookhaven would do.

"That's a good idea. I'll do that," Sage replied.

I thought about asking her about the footage. Only it would seem out of nowhere and if I wanted her to be honest with me, it needed to feel natural in the conversation. It could keep until later. I ended the call. Absolved of that particular obligation, maybe now I could find a way to give myself some peace of mind. Even though I still had that big gap in my memory, I was coming around to the notion that if anything, I was being set up. I didn't know why anyone would want to blame me for Vera's death, but it fueled me forward.

'*Library.*'

Beau's suggestion made sense. It was close by and probably had private cubicles and computers that wouldn't track my browser history. Time to find out just who McKenzie Lawson was and why someone would want her dead.

10

The library sat adjacent to the public school on Center Street. It ran parallel to Main Street. A sign at the front read 'Brookhaven K-12' suggesting that students of all ages attended in one place. School wasn't in session thanks to the summer holiday, but I spotted a children's play area behind tall wire fencing occupied by a couple of kids chasing each other around the swing set as their mothers watched from a nearby bench. None of them paid me any mind as I crossed the grass strewn path from the school proper to the library.

Inside, it looked like what I imagined all American public libraries did. A single desk at the front staffed by a matronly woman with glasses perched on the end of her nose and rows upon rows of carefully cataloged books and other media.

"Afternoon," the librarian whose name plate read Gladys greeted me.

"Hi. I was hoping you might have some public computers available?"

She eyed me over the rim of her glasses and pointed to the bulge in my pocket where my phone sat. "That not working?"

"Oh, um yeah. It's just that reading's a bit easier on a bigger screen. And my Wi-Fi connection's a bit wobbly today," I answered.

She seemed to buy my explanation and gestured to a short corridor to my left leading to a wide open area lined with small cubicles along the walls. Each was equipped with a desktop computer that looked mercifully like it had been purchased in the last half decade. The space was filled by a handful of adults with packs tucked under their feet. A balding man sat in an overstuffed armchair in one corner reading a newspaper three months out of date.

I gave him a polite nod to acknowledge his presence before retreating to a cubicle in the corner opposite the door. I didn't expect anyone to be watching me, but I couldn't be too careful. If I didn't think it would freak the other patrons out, I would have tried to convince Beau to turn us both invisible via his camouflage. Except the bloke in the chair knew I was here so that wasn't an option.

"Okay, time to go digging," I whispered under my breath, even though it would have had the same effect if I'd thought it loudly to Beau.

After clicking through an annoying number of statements that what I viewed was not really private and that having thrice agreed not to watch pornography, I gained access to the library's internet connection.

I started with a general web search of Vera Chase. I figured I would start with who she said she was when she got here. It came up with an Instagram account and a Facebook profile. The photo that displayed when I followed the link to the Facebook account matched Vera, albeit a slightly younger version of her. She hadn't updated her photo in some time.

"No shame in that," I noted to no one in particular. It was a flattering picture of her too, so I could understand not wanting to change it.

I clicked around the page, noting the sparsity of her information. It listed a birthday which I couldn't confirm or deny as being real. The account had been active for years, but the latest update was more than six months ago. It was marked as New Year's Eve and showed Vera in a revealing dress, sitting in the lap of a guy she was clearly flirting with. He didn't seem to mind it, although he had managed to only get his face in profile. He had dark hair and scruff on his chin. I couldn't quite bring myself to classify it as a beard or even a five o'clock shadow, but he did bear a resemblance to the bearded man I'd seen at Ginny's the day Vera arrived. I scrolled up to the basic bio information again. Her hometown wasn't listed although as I scrolled through the photos, some of them were geotagged in New York City. Enough of them bore that tag that I had to assume that's where she'd come from. Plus, she had told us she'd been looking to get away from city life.

"What were you doing in New York that brought you here and yet your trouble followed?"

I skimmed through the expansive list of friends on Vera's account, but none even appeared as close friends or relatives. At most, they were acquaintances, like she'd accepted connection requests from anyone who asked. She had to have people in her life that would come looking for her. I couldn't believe anyone in Brookhaven would want her dead.

I focused on the photos, taking note of anyone else tagged with her. A half dozen people cropped up in a handful of photos each, some in groups and others in pairs. I spotted one of her and a guy standing beside her with one arm wrapped around her shoulders. Too bad he wasn't tagged. Though he looked similar to the guy she'd been sprawled over in the New Year's photograph. I picked the same face out of a few other photos she'd posted as well. They always looked suitably intimate, so I had to assume he was her boyfriend. Something about his face raised signals in the back of my mind. There was something familiar about his penetrating gaze that made me think of the man from Ginny's, but we'd not even interacted. It was probably my mind playing tricks on me.

This wasn't what I'd expected when I started my search. For all intents and purposes, Vera Chase was a real person with a social life, even if she'd fallen off the map months ago. Plenty of people went ages without posting updates.

"What am I missing?" I grumbled.

I opened a second tab, repeated my search, and navigated to the Instagram page. More photos populated the page—many of which were duplicates from her Facebook account. She seemed to be more eager to keep this platform updated, because I found posts from as recent as a month ago on her feed. It was mostly her with various cityscapes behind her, but there was one where she had flashed her left hand at the camera as the sun glinted off a ring. The glare aside, I could make out an array of diamonds and maybe an emerald or two adorning her finger. It was gaudy and noticeable— screamed 'look how wealthy my fiancé is.'

She didn't have an engagement ring when she got here. It was big and ornate and not easily concealed.

'Check the room.'

"Easier said than done," I muttered under my breath. "If it was in her room at the B&B, it's in police custody now."

I drummed my fingers on the keys, trying to figure out my next move. There were other results on the page from my search on Vera, but I'd been so focused on the social media, I hadn't thought to look. I hit the back button on the browser tab I was in and skimmed through the results. There were no news articles about her being missing or having another identity or who might be looking for her. That would have been too easy.

I left the page open and brought up a third tab, doing a search this time for McKenzie Lawson. This query brought up a single Facebook page. It, too, was set to public thankfully and I could see that she had a paltry list of friends. Only one or two were listed as close friends or relatives. She listed her hometown as Albany, New York. She had even fewer posts than Vera's page, the last of which was a belated birthday post from someone named Walter Lawson four months ago. The fact they shared the same last name suggested some sort of familial link. A check of her friends list identified him as her brother. I clicked on his name in the post, but his page was set to private, and I couldn't see anything useful beyond that he was McKenzie's brother.

I leaned back in the chair and felt Beau's claws disengage from my shoulder. He trundled down my left arm to perch on the desk. I rubbed the spot he'd occupied, feeling the tiny scratches he'd left behind. If chameleons could glare, he was giving me a major stink eye.

"I didn't say a word," I hissed.

Staring at the page and flipping between the other tabs open didn't offer up anything useful. It wasn't like Vera had started one page and then created the other when she decided to switch identities. Both pages had been in existence for a long time. The fact that both hadn't been updated in months was curious, but there was obviously a piece of the puzzle missing. And it wasn't one I was going to figure out sitting here staring at a screen.

"So, where to now?" I sighed.

'Brother. Look deeper.'

I flipped back to McKenzie's page and studied the tiny image of Walter. I wasn't sure what I was supposed to do with his photo. I hadn't seen him before, had I? I went back through McKenzie's photo albums and did a search for Walter being tagged in them. There were a few from a couple years ago. They looked happy, mugging for the camera. They grew more distant as time passed. He was in fewer photos, but the more I looked at him, the more I felt like I'd seen him before. That seemed impossible as I'd never been to Albany, or anywhere outside of Brookhaven since I'd gotten to the States. But something about his face—the pinched look around his eyes and mouth, and the pale green of his eyes were familiar. He could have been the man on the pier I'd seen this afternoon.

"Okay, I don't know where I'm supposed to look for this guy."

Beau flicked his tail so fast I wasn't sure it had actually moved. But when I looked back at the screen, the search results for McKenzie were back up. Of course, what an idiot I was. Just because I hadn't found anything else out about Vera from my search this way, didn't mean I wouldn't about McKenzie. I didn't have to scroll past the third listing to find a newspaper in a small New York town offering advertisements and classifieds. One mentioned McKenzie by name. I navigated to the page and scanned the brief blurb accompanied by a small color photo of McKenzie that looked like it had been pulled from her Facebook page and cropped.

Seeking missing sister. Twenty-four-year-old McKenzie Lawson was last seen in upstate New York. She disappeared late Thursday evening after a public gathering with friends. If you have any information, please visit the following website, and contact me. Kenz, if you're out there, please come home. – Walter Lawson, concerned brother.

The pet name he'd used suddenly clicked in my memory. That was the name the customer had called Vera. I followed the link embedded in the blurb which came up with a crudely designed website with the same photo of McKenzie along with some more details about her height, weight, and hair color. I could see Walter had set up a way for people to leave messages on the website to contact him. There were mostly messages of concern and support, posters telling Walter they hoped he found his missing sister. There were a couple of comments from the last month that pointed him toward Massachusetts. Had it been Walter I'd seen and overheard arguing with Vera before she was murdered?

Even if it had been, it didn't explain why he would have killed her. From the little I could discern from his hunt, he was just trying to bring his sister home safe. That was a far cry from strangling her.

'Seek him out,' Beau offered in my head.

"How?" I whispered.

'Message him.'

Well, there was an idea. I clicked the button to post a new comment, but an error message appeared, noting that the plug-in had been shut off by the site administrator. I searched the rest of the web page, hoping for a mobile number or an email address, but nothing came up.

"That's a bust. I'll have to try and find him here, but I've no idea where to even look for him. It's not like he'd have reason to come back to High Time now that she's dead. I'd have better luck trying to look for that ring," I posited softly.

"Someone's being naughty." Sam's lyrical voice came from directly behind me.

I tried not to startle too obviously. I cast a look over my left shoulder to find the man still reading his out-of-date newspaper, although he peered at me over top of it. None of the other patrons using computers appeared interested in me. I swallowed and pulled my phone from my pocket and pressed it to my ear.

"There's no phones in here," he said, gesturing to a sign posted by the door.

At least he didn't think I was mental for talking to myself.

"Sorry," I said and cleared the search history and closed the browser. Beau slipped up my arm as I left the cubicle behind, and he seemed gentler as he clung on this time.

I wasn't ready to leave the library yet. I needed a plan of action. Pausing by the front desk to thank the librarian for her help, I made my way into the stacks of meticulously organized books and found a large plush chair in one corner of the children's section. It was empty and I sat down.

"Right, so you don't approve of my idea," I said, addressing Sam who'd floated along unseen as I found some privacy.

"Oh, no, I love the idea. I did always like a bit of a bad girl," he said with a wistful sigh. "Not romantically, mind you, but ..." he trailed off. "Not the point. Do you have a plan for this daring little bit of detective work?"

"Well, I don't suppose you can turn corporeal and let me in the back door?"

"No such luck." He studied his manicured nails. "These beauties haven't been able to touch solid things in decades. But you know no one locks their doors around here."

"That's rubbish. Course they do," I scoffed, remembering to hold my phone to my ear in case anyone came through.

"Maybe they did in London or wherever, but this is Brookhaven. Being trusting is practically a small town requirement."

"But, surely Chief Hayes would have locked up when he was done going through everything."

"Nope. Both doors are still wide open."

"Just so I'm not crazy, the name you saw on the ID, could it have been McKenzie?"

He tapped his chin in contemplation for a moment. "Could have been."

"And you didn't happen to notice if they found anything like jewelry in her room?"

"I wasn't really interested in the stuff they were going through," he retorted, making it abundantly clear by the leering look he gave me that he'd been far more interested in the *people* doing the searching.

"Right. Well, if we're going to do this, it better be soon. While everyone else is still at work."

"Don't you think you ought to loop in Tania?" Sam pressed.

"I'll let her know if I find anything," I said.

In reality, I knew she was hiding something. There had to be a reason she hadn't told me she'd spoken with Vera—or McKenzie—and that I had to hear it from Maggie. Whatever I was going to find in the house could be that reason. Until I knew what it was, I was going to keep this little adventure to myself.

"Come on. We've got some snooping to do."

11

Getting from the library back to the B&B didn't take long. I really had to appreciate how close everything was in this town. Unfortunately, as I walked up the street toward my destination, I spotted cars in driveways and televisions turned on in front rooms of the houses directly abutting Tania's.

"Maybe I should just come back later," I said to Sam as he bobbed in mid-air beside me.

"Don't tell me you're getting cold feet," he whined.

"No, but there's people at home. That means witnesses," I hissed even though none of the townsfolk could hear me.

"Well, gee, if only you knew someone who could

camouflage you," Sam snorted, pressing his hand to his face in an obnoxious gesture.

Using Beau's magic to hide me hadn't occurred to me, despite my earlier wish at the library that he could have used it on me. I felt pressure on my right shoulder.

"What do you think mate? You up for hiding me? Just long enough to get inside," I said, reaching up to run a finger along the scales on the top of his head.

'Be safer.'

He seemed in agreement with the plan, so I waited for his magic to wash over me. It was a strange sensation, like warming up from the inside while being washed over with cool water. It was a pleasant sensation, if one that didn't quite make sense.

I looked down and blinked as my hand came in and out of focus. It seemed to be working as I crept up the drive and around the back of the house. I hadn't been out in the back garden much since I'd moved in. Still, it was plausible that my fingerprints could be on the door handle. I took precaution anyway, wrapping my hand in the hem of my shirt before tugging the door open.

As Sam had predicted, the door was unlocked. It opened into a small room that sat directly behind the large kitchen. Out of habit, I slid off my shoes and proceeded in my socks. The kitchen was eerily disorganized. They hadn't given Tania time to clean up the food she'd been making. She normally kept such a pristine cooking space. I leaned an elbow on the counter and eyed the spoiled food in the pot. I wanted to discard it so my friend wouldn't have to come home to such a mess, but then I remembered I wasn't supposed to be here. The same sensation of warming and cooling hit me, but in reverse as Beau dropped his invisibility from around me.

I marched without preamble upstairs to Vera's room. The bed was unmade, the mattress askew like someone had lifted it up to check beneath it. If I were hiding something like another identity, that would be where I might have hidden it, too.

"Sam, you're going to need to help me. Where did they find the other ID?"

"In the nightstand. Girl really thought her secrets would be safe there."

I retreated to my room long enough to pull on one of the only cardigans I'd brought with me. I would be sweating soon, but it gave me some cover for my hands rather than the hem of my shirt. I eased open the drawer to the nightstand, but found it empty. I shouldn't have expected to find anything in there, especially if the police had already made a sweep through it.

"If I were hiding an insanely expensive engagement ring, where would I put it?" I wondered aloud.

"If you're smart, a safety deposit box," Sam retorted. "If you're in a small town, in the bathroom."

I eyed him skeptically. "No one actually hides things in their sanitary products. You know that, right?"

"I didn't say they did. Besides, I'd check the toilet first."

Stepping into the hallway, I paused, trying to think if I'd seen her spend a long time in the bathroom. Nothing like that came to mind, except for her initial day when she'd arrived. I hadn't noticed the ring on her. Though she'd gone upstairs with her bag quickly and I'd left before she'd come back down. Plenty of time to hide the ring then, and without the questioning looks of people who knew of its existence. It's hard to ask about something you don't know is important.

"This is going to be unpleasant," I groaned as I crossed the hall into the bathroom. I hiked up the sleeves of my cardigan and lifted off the top of the toilet tank. The water burbled within, but there was no obvious sign of anything hidden in its depths.

"You're going to have to get wet, honey," Sam nudged.

"Sure you don't want to have a go? Maybe you'd actually get to touch something solid," I offered.

"Not that I wouldn't love some snazzy bling, but it's not really what I had in mind if I ever got the chance. Come on, put your big girl pants on."

Swallowing back my nerves, I dunked my right hand into the chilly water, groping along the bottom of the tank and around the pipes inside feeding water to the fixture.

"Nothing," I huffed and pulled my hand out. I flipped on the hot water tap and scrubbed my hand for good measure before drying my hands. "What if we're thinking about this wrong? What if she didn't have the ring, because she broke it off with the fiancé? Maybe that's why she took off and her brother's chasing her?"

"Or maybe she sold it?" Sam suggested.

With the number of stones it had, I could imagine she'd get a pretty penny for it, even from a small town pawnbroker. But the police hadn't mentioned anything about finding cash in her belongings. And there was no way she would have spent it all in a week.

"Guess I'd better go pay the pawn shop a visit," I said.

Sam blipped out of sight, rematerializing as if to block the way. "Not without an offering. Tyson doesn't talk to people snooping around. He's been burned by bad deals in the past."

"It's not like I've got anything worth selling," I argued.

"Tania keeps the good silver in the top drawer by the stove," Sam noted.

"I'm not stealing Tania's silver to follow a lead that may go nowhere," I scoffed. "Can't I just go in, show him a photo of the ring, and ask how much he thinks it would be worth? Or say I'm here to buy something? That would give me a chance to see if he's even got it."

"I'm telling you, having something shiny to distract him is worth its weight in gold."

I closed my eyes and inhaled through my nose and out through my mouth. There was one thing I could use, so long as I was able to get it back. My parents may have basically disowned me the moment I told them I had magic, but my gran had still talked to me. She'd given me a pendant she'd said had been passed down through her side of the family for generations. Which meant it had some monetary value.

"Fine, I've got something I can use, but if I can't get it back when this is over, I'm going to find a way to resurrect you and kill you all over again," I threatened.

"You aren't the first to say that," he called in a sing-song voice as I returned to my room long enough to discard the cardigan and pocket the pendant. Its weight seemed twice as heavy in my pocket as I crept back downstairs, retracing my steps through the first floor.

'Flowers.'

Beau's voice was jarring in my head, forcing me to stop walking. He'd dislodged himself earlier and I'd barely noticed. I checked both my shoulders, but he hadn't reappeared there. So, where was he hiding now?

"Can you be a bit more specific?" I called out.

A tingling sensation filled my belly and my feet moved of their own volition, leading me to the dining room and a flowerpot sitting on a table beside the large windows facing the back of the property. Beau sat curled around the base of the pot. The flowers in the ceramic looked strange, waxy. I ran my fingers over the petals and the leaves, and leaned in to take a whiff.

"Fake?"

Tania had plenty of live plants in the house. I wasn't entirely convinced she hadn't gotten more before my arrival just to help me hone my skills. So, why would she keep fake flowers in a pot by a window that got great sunlight?

"This is weird," I murmured and picked up the flowerpot, careful not to send Beau toppling.

The vessel itself was ceramic and sturdy, but not overly heavy. So, why did the whole thing carry more heft than it should? I tugged the flowers and Styrofoam soil free, setting them on the table before peering inside.

"Bloody hell."

"Share with the rest of us," Sam said.

I tipped the pot all the way vertical and shook. When nothing happened, I reached a hand in and freed the bottleneck. Wads of bundled bills fell onto the small table, sending Beau skittering out of the way. Beside me, Sam let out a low whistle.

"What kind of stones did you say that ring had?"

"Emeralds and diamonds. Decent sized ones."

I wasn't great with American currency, but I believed there were several thousand dollars here.

Maybe close to one hundred thousand. Was it possible the ring had been worth that much to Tyson the pawnbroker? Did he have that kind of cash on hand?

If Vera had in fact paid him a visit to sell the ring, it was possible though, because whatever led her to Brookhaven meant she hadn't had enough money to pay Tania's modest rental fee. But why on earth would she hide it in plain sight? It also begged the question, did Tania know about the money?

"I wouldn't leave that lying around," Sam said, dispelling my thoughts.

"Right." I stuffed the cash back into the pot, replaced the fake flowers and set the arrangement back on the table.

I needed to make a trip to the pawn shop, and I needed to find Tania. One or both of them might have answers that I could bring to Chief Hayes. Or maybe Vinnie, given how directly the chief had told me to stay out of his investigation.

'Vigilance.'

Beau's one-word warning sent shivers down my spine and as if on instinct, I looked out the window. The grass was fenced in on two sides, separating Tania's property from her neighbors, but I thought I spotted movement at the far left corner. Did someone see me? I'd been so careful to make sure no one saw me enter the house. It hadn't occurred to me that anyone might be snooping around the back of the house.

I held an arm out for Beau. "You better come with me. It won't do if people see me leaving the house, but never saw me enter."

Tyson's Treasures sat at the edge of town closest to the highway. Whether it had been a conscious choice to lure in potential customers or the luck of the draw on the real estate, it sat off Main Street, in a spot where the rest of the town could quietly forget it existed.

The tiny gold bell above the door rang, announcing my presence as I stepped inside. The air had a heady quality to it, like he was burning incense or something. I remembered what Sam had said about Tyson being the receiver of bad deals in the past. Had he gotten caught up in receiving stolen goods? Or had he just sold the wrong person's family heirloom? The front of the shop was cramped, with just enough room for a display case atop which the register sat. The owner was nowhere to be seen.

Granted, I had no frame of reference for what Tyson looked like.

"Hello?" I called out, hoping my voice would make Tyson materialize.

I waited in the small space in silence, my voice oddly reverberating in my ears keeping me company. Beau had gone off as soon as I was clear of the B&B, so I didn't even have him by my side. Finally, the air around me grew heavy, like a pressure front coming in right before a storm. It made my temples ache and my ears popped.

Then, a slender man with dark skin and an eye patch covering his left eye appeared. He wore a button-down dress shirt and slacks. He looked far too well dressed to be selling questionable goods. But maybe that was the point and he was well-dressed to disarm his customers. Make them feel like he was more legit.

"You're looking for something, young lady," he said, his voice gravelly.

"Uh, maybe." I dug the pendant out of my pocket. "I'm a bit strapped for cash and I was wondering how much I might be able to get for this?"

He held out a hand and I noticed how smooth the pads of his fingers and his palm were as he accepted the pendant. He cradled it between his fingers. "You sure you want to part with this?"

"Wouldn't if I had any other choice," I said. It wasn't a lie.

"Indeed." He reached behind the counter and retrieved a small case. Opening it revealed a soft velvety interior. "Give me a moment."

He set the pendant down gently and retreated from view again. With my luck, the man had magic, too. Would have been nice for Sam to warn me about that. I was beginning to suspect most people had some sort of supernatural gift in this town.

I took a step back to study the display case in front of me. I doubted he kept everything he received here. But people did come to pawn shops as shoppers, not just sellers. I didn't see the ring at first glance.

Tyson cleared his throat as he returned and set about studying the pendant. "It's in remarkable condition. Looks to be at least seventy or eighty years old." He shined a light on it and rubbed it with a small cloth. "Silver by the looks of it."

"So, what's that get me?"

He let out a sigh. "I could give you four hundred for it."

I had no idea if that was lowballing it or not. I

had no intention of actually parting with it. "I can't accept less than seven," I lied.

He passed it back to me. "Then I'm afraid I'm not the man to do business with."

I slid the pendant back into my pocket and was about to leave, feeling defeated when an idea presented itself to me. With Tyson's back turned, I pulled out my phone, typed in Vera's handle on Instagram and pulled up the photo of her flashing the engagement ring. I double tapped it to enlarge it.

"What about this?"

He leaned toward the phone. "Hard to say without seeing it in person."

"It belonged to someone who died. I think it had a few carats worth of diamonds and emeralds. That's got to be worth more than four hundred."

"More than seven, too," he replied. "Like I said, I'd have to see it, but just based on that picture, I'd say probably worth three thousand. Once I verify, I could probably give you twenty-five hundred."

Nothing close to one hundred grand.

There was no way he would quote me something over ninety thousand dollars less than what I'd found stashed in the vase, even if he planned to resell it at a higher value. He was probably telling the truth and that meant Vera hadn't pawned the ring. If she had an acrimonious split from her partner, she could have tossed the ring in his face, but that just didn't feel right.

"I'll think about it."

"Don't wait too long, if you're that strapped for money," he said.

"I don't have the ring. But if something that looks like it comes in, can you let me know?"

He gave a dismissive snort. "I don't discuss my other customers' business. Either you bring me the ring, or don't."

I stowed my phone back in my pocket and left the shop. My stomach burbled with hunger. It had been longer than I'd realized since lunch and I was hungry. My phone buzzed with a text from Maggie, inviting me over for dinner. I started on my way back to her flat, but stopped in front of Ginny's. I felt the tiny hairs on my arms stand up like they were electrically charged.

I didn't hide my paranoia as I spun around, ready to confront whoever was watching me. Only a handful of people populated the street, and none appeared to notice me. A man stood studying his phone across the road and he rubbed at the stubble on his chin. I hurried along, eager to be inside and up a floor, away from prying eyes.

12

The scent of sizzling bacon greeted me when I walked into Maggie's living room. If Sam were here, he would have probably taunted me about everyone leaving their doors unlocked. My host stood in the kitchen, griddle on one side and a pan of frying meat on the stove.

"Is Tania joining us?"

Maggie looked over her shoulder at me. "Once she's done at the station."

"So, you called Vinnie?"

"No. I called Tania and suggested she might want to share whatever information she had with Rick."

"Oh ..." After a beat, I added, "You didn't have to cook."

She laughed. "I know I'm not the culinary whizz that Tania is, but I can cook up a decent breakfast."

"For dinner?"

Another laugh. "Live in this country long enough and you'll learn that breakfast for dinner is a staple in some households."

"Can I help?"

She pointed to a bowl of batter. "Stir that for me and then spoon some onto the griddle." She held her hand over the flat surface. "Yeah, that should be good to go."

I did as instructed. After giving the batter a good clockwise whorl, I spooned out four decent sized pools onto the griddle. The batter sizzled almost as loudly as the bacon in the pan. I watched as tiny bubbles formed on the surface.

"So, I know we left things kind of awkward at lunch," I began, intending to apologize for pushing her to talk to the police.

"Don't worry about it. I get that you're concerned about the investigation. Especially with Rick focusing his attention on you."

"He thought you might have given me something to heal wounds on my hands. The killer used a vine to strangle Vera and it had prickers," I volunteered.

"For all he touts hating Ginny's gossip mill, he's not above using it to his advantage," she grumbled.

"I did a little digging into Vera, thanks to Sam's little tip," I added as Maggie handed me a spatula. I started to work it under the pancakes, loosening them bit by bit until I could flip them without making a giant mess.

"I thought he didn't catch the name," Maggie noted, using tongs to pull the bacon from the pan before setting it on a plate draped with a cloth.

"He didn't. But while I was at the station, I happened to catch a glimpse of the name on her other ID. I did some light Facebook stalking," I explained.

"And what did you find?"

"Honestly, I'm not sure. She had two accounts, one under each name. Both seemed to go dormant within the last few months. There's maybe a brother looking for her. And ..." I leaned in closer, "She had a fiancé. Gave her a massive rock, but it's not in her belongings."

Before Maggie could respond, the door opened and Tania walked in. She didn't look at all bothered by her trip to the station. Maybe whatever she'd been unwilling to tell me had come out under Chief Hayes' scrutiny.

"Maggie is making breakfast for dinner I see," Tania said as if she didn't have a care in the world.

"Those pancakes are good to come off now," Maggie said, drawing my attention to the griddle in front of me.

"What? Oh, sorry." I slid the pancakes off and gave the batter another stir before putting four more on to cook. Tania settled on the couch and watched Maggie and me. Did she know I knew she'd been the last person to see Vera—or was it, McKenzie—alive?

"Darcy was just telling me about some information she came across," Maggie said, giving me no option but to come clean to Tania. Maybe if I came clean, she would, too.

"What's that then?" Tania asked, brushing graying strands behind her ears.

"Well, I think Vera had another identity. One where she was engaged to a guy in New York."

"I never saw any ring," Tania noted.

"Neither did I. And I went looking." I probably shouldn't have admitted I'd gone back to the house. Still, I'd been careful.

"She mentioned she was upset about something the day she died," Tania added.

"So, you admit you talked to her then?" I blurted.

She sat back and stared at me. "I never said I hadn't."

"But you talked to her after I did. I told you I was freaking out about that gap in my memory. And you could have at least told me you'd seen her after she left High Time."

"I'm sorry I didn't mention it sooner. I was still in shock. You may have been the one to find her, and we might not have known her very long, but you weren't the only one who'd formed an attachment."

"The missing ring wasn't the only thing I discovered. She's got a brother, or at least her other identity does, who is looking for her."

"Maybe that's who you heard her arguing with?" Maggie offered from the kitchen. "Didn't you say he called her another name?"

Kenz. Short for McKenzie.

"She insisted she didn't know him and that wasn't her name. If she was running from him, that could make sense," I agreed. Though it still didn't get me any closer to finding out if he'd killed her.

Time for the money question.

I turned to Tania, looked her straight in the eye and said, "Did you know there's like one hundred grand in the house?"

"What?" Color drained from her cheeks, and she looked away. "There is no chance that's right."

"I talked to Tyson, and he quoted me twenty-five hundred for the ring if she'd pawned it. I don't know, maybe she pawned it before she left New York. But that money is definitely there."

"This is the first I'm hearing of it." Tania's voice was strained.

"Dinner's up," Maggie called, cutting my questioning short.

If only Beau was here to tell me what Tania was hiding. She had been so supportive of me coming back to town and offering me a place to live. But she was keeping secrets and I couldn't understand why.

I settled at the table across from Maggie and did my best to not let the feeling stew and fester within me. It wasn't like Tania, and I were best mates who told each other everything. There were things about her life I didn't know and had no reason to, and there were things about mine I wasn't ready to share with her..

Dinner passed quickly enough and I excused myself to the bathroom. I lingered, hoping my absence might get Tania to talk to Maggie. As I started to wash my hands, my lingering paid off.

"You don't have to keep everything so close," Maggie argued.

"It's my business," Tania replied.

"You know all you need to do is ask and the people of this town will do anything they can." Maggie's voice rose in volume.

Tania made a scoffing sound and I heard the clatter of a cup hitting the counter. *What did Maggie find out*? I opened the bathroom door, stepping into the living room to find my landlady and our hostess talking by the stove. Dishes from our meal sat in the sink under sudsy water.

"Sorry, didn't mean to shout," Maggie said the instant she saw me.

"Is everything okay?"

Tania just gave me a wordless nod. We were in the not talking to each other phase apparently. It wasn't like I'd accused her of murder or anything. I mean, for one thing I didn't think she had a mean bone in her body. I couldn't see her killing someone. Besides even if she had, it was foolish to leave the body in her own car.

"Here, let me do the dishes," I offered, shooing the other women into the living room.

As I stood at the sink, I started to form a plan of action. Someone had been following me, I knew that. And yet no one had come to claim Vera's body that I had heard of. If McKenzie's brother really was in town looking for her, surely he'd have come forward by now? Yet, no one was talking about him. I needed to find him. Brookhaven wasn't that big a town. If he'd come to the dispensary once, maybe I'd get lucky, and he'd come again. There weren't any other hotels in town that I was aware of, so he had to be staying someplace nearby.

Twenty minutes later, the dishes were done and I'd managed the beginnings of a plan. It would unfortunately involve talking to Ginny Hayes and relying on her knack for oversharing with anyone who would listen—and some who wouldn't. But it would have to wait until morning. I had the morning off, which gave me plenty of time to camp out at Ginny's.

"Thank you again for dinner, but we should be going," Tania announced. Maggie stood beside me at the sink, still nursing a cup of coffee while I stayed rooted to the spot in the living room.

"You two are always welcome," Maggie pulled Tania in for a quick hug.

Tania turned to me. "Well, I suppose your night doesn't have to end yet."

I barely stifled a yawn. "No, I think a good night's

sleep is what I need." To Maggie, I said, "Thanks again for all your help."

Maggie wordlessly pulled me into a tight embrace. She held fast and whispered, "Keep looking for answers."

I smiled in spite of myself. For whatever reason, she was pushing me to find the truth, no matter where it led me.

I joined Tania at street level and we walked down Main Street in silence. I wanted to tell her that I was sorry for making her feel as if I'd been accusing her, but I couldn't bring myself to say the words.

The B&B looked inviting in the late night air. The neighbors' porch lights cast it in a warm amber glow. We both stopped in the foyer. The front room was a mess. I hadn't paid much mind to it on my exploration earlier, but I was certain the couch cushions had been in their proper place.

"This wasn't Rick and Vinnie," Tania breathed.

I pushed past her into the kitchen. It was still a mild mess, but nothing appeared out of sorts compared to this afternoon. I could see broken glass in the back door at hand height. Clearly whoever had come in hadn't realized the door was open. If they'd been watching me, maybe they'd assumed I had a key. Walter or Vera's fiancé were from out of town. They probably didn't realize that no one locked their doors.

"*Dios, mio!*" Tania moaned upon seeing the glass strewn all over the floor.

I didn't spot any flecks of red that would indicate the intruder had cut themselves or left any useful evidence for the police to find.

I moved into the dining room and my stomach lurched. The flowerpot with the fake flowers had been smashed into shards on the floor. The flowers lay discarded and the money was gone.

13

"We need to call the police," Tania said, her voice shaky.

She wasn't wrong. Someone had very obviously broken in and stolen the money. I turned to give my landlady a curt look. "I think maybe we ought to discuss the money first."

Tania's shoulders sagged and she sank deflated into a chair. "I don't know what's gotten into me. Honestly. I think maybe I was embarrassed."

"I mean I suppose that's a natural reaction, lying to people who you are supposed to trust," I noted.

"Not about that. Yes I feel bad for not telling you the truth. But you have to understand, this place has been my family's life since before I was born."

"I know. You told me your parents built it when they came from Argentina."

"Times have changed since they opened it. The world is changing. People aren't coming to stay here like they used to." She waved her hand around. "I'm sure you have noticed that aside from you and Vera, there are no other guests."

"So, you were hiding money?" I replied.

"No. When Vera arrived, she said she could pay me more than I asked. She said she wasn't sure how long she was going to be staying, but she just gave me stacks of bills."

"And you took it?" I continued flatly.

"That kind of money would keep the B&B open for a long time."

"So why leave it in a flowerpot? I mean, why not take it to the bank?"

"I was going to, in small batches. Otherwise, it would look suspicious."

"Did she say where she'd gotten it from?"

Tania shook her head. "I didn't ask. I could tell she was running from something, and I didn't want to press her. Not before she was ready."

"Is that what you were talking to her about the day she died?"

"No. She said she was upset, because someone

had approached her at the dispensary. It had her worried."

Her brother. "Did she explain why she was worried?"

"Just that she thought someone else might be looking for her. She didn't say more than that. I told her to go talk to Rick if she had concerns about her safety. I don't think she did."

"Thank you for telling me," I said, sitting in the seat beside her.

"*Gracias* for being so understanding. I know you've been in a tough spot yourself."

"I think I was followed earlier today. I was careful getting into the house thanks to Beau, but I let him drop his camouflage when we were inside. I didn't think anyone would see. But I swear someone was watching me when I found the money. I think it was whoever is trying to make it look like I killed Vera."

"And is trying to pit us against each other," she noted.

"Well, they aren't going to get away with it."

She squeezed my hand as tears slid down her cheeks. "No, they won't."

After a beat, she dried her eyes with the back of her free hand and stood up. "I'm going to call Rick and let him know there's been a break-in."

"Doesn't that mean you have to tell him about the money?" I prompted.

"I told him that she'd paid me in advance for some of her stay. I did not say how much."

"Hey, Sam, are you around?" I called.

No answer.

"He likes to spend his evenings and early mornings by the pier. He says the sunset and sunrise remind him of being alive," Tania told me.

"Should we go to the pier and see if he saw anything?"

"If I know Sam, which I like to think I do by now, he'd have been out long before whoever broke in."

Beau!

"What about Beau? He could have seen something. Or heard something, sensed someone in the house," I continued.

Tania shook her head. "He was at Maggie's with us." She paused. "But I know something that was here that might be able to lead us to where we need to go."

"And that would be?"

"The plants. Especially the ones in the back where they broke in."

"Why didn't I think of that?" Maybe, because my

magic was so unreliable, I wasn't confident I could get the plants to tell me a bloody thing.

"Go out back now while I call Rick. You'll have ten minutes at most to see what you can find."

I started for the back door before thinking better of it. I didn't need to trample the crime scene. So, I retraced my steps out the front and went around the back to stand amidst the grass. I doubted the neighbors had seen or heard anything. They certainly didn't have cameras pointing this way to provide video surveillance. I gave the door a wide berth and trailed along the back of the building until I came to stand outside the window with a direct view into the dining room. It was too tall for me to reach, but gauging by the photos I'd seen of McKenzie and her brother, Walter was likely tall enough to reach the window without too much trouble. Vera's fiancé could have been, too. Still, if either of them had been watching me, they'd know where the money was. Why bother going in the back door? Why not smash the window right here?

I knocked against the glass and realized it was double paned. Smashing it from this side wouldn't have guaranteed the inner pane would shatter, too. And it would leave two layers of glass to crawl through.

I noticed muddy indentations in the ground beneath the window. Our thief had considered this spot long enough to leave impressions in the earth. They'd trampled grass in their wake as they tracked to the door to do their breaking and entering. It was too dark to make out much without artificial light and I turned on my phone's flashlight to confirm there were in fact tread marks in the dirt.

I knelt on the grass and closed my eyes. Breathing in slowly, I took in the rich scent of fresh grass and dirt beneath my fingers. *It should want to tell me what happened.* After all, in a way, someone had hurt this spot, too.

No whispers bounced around in the back of my mind. *Come on, work.*

I stood and brushed off the grass stains from my fingers. I was about to retreat when I noticed dark vines looping up the far fence near our neighbors on the right. I took careful steps to avoid contaminating the scene and studied the plants hanging there. They looked like the one used to strangle Vera. I poked a finger at one of the strands and winced as the tiny barb bit into the sensitive flesh of my fingertip. Well, Chief Hayes was right, whoever had used this likely would have cut themselves in the process. I traced the undulating loops of greenery along the fence toward the back edge of the property until I got to a spot where there was a deliberate break in the vine. Someone had cut the length of it from here. Someone who was trying to frame either me or Tania. I suspected they didn't care which of us took the law enforcement's attention.

I still couldn't quite put that manipulative intent together with either Walter or Vera's fiancé. I couldn't even be certain I'd seen either of them in town, although I did feel pretty sure it had been Walter I'd seen on the pier at lunchtime. I really needed to talk to him myself. Which meant I needed to pray he came back to High Time while I was there. I doubted he'd fixed the messaging plug-in on his website, and he would have no reason to accept a random friend request from me.

The whine of police sirens filled the air and I retreated back around the side of the house to stand outside on the front porch. Tania joined me as Rick and Vinnie climbed out of the cruiser.

"You really think you've been robbed?" Chief Hayes' tone dripped with skepticism.

"Unless the two of you left my home in shambles," Tania countered pithily.

I couldn't keep my snort from escaping. The chief glared at me, his brown eyes flashing with that eerie touch of amber they often did. It was even more noticeable in the dark. He made a 'lead the way' gesture and Tania pivoted to usher them inside. I followed last. We stopped in the living room first.

"Have you checked to see if anything is missing?" Vinnie asked.

"Honestly, no. I called as soon as we got here and found it this way," Tania answered.

Not exactly the truth, but it would give us time to look for any other missing items. Chief Hayes let out an exasperated sigh before pulling out a notepad and addressing his deputy.

"Vinnie, go up with Ms. Ingram, see if any of her belongings are missing. I'll take a statement from Tania and go over things down here."

That left me out of the money discussion. Good. Vinnie led the way and stopped at the top of the stairs.

"Should we check all the rooms?" I asked.

"We'll start with the occupied ones and go from there. Rick will go over Tania's. So, let's start in your room."

"Right."

I went first, walking into room number four. At least I'd remembered to make the bed. The mattress was askew and some of my clothes had been strewn on the floor in the closet. I knelt on the floor to go through my things. I couldn't imagine anyone would take my belongings unless they wanted to somehow plant evidence.

"Anything missing?" Vinnie called from the doorway.

"Still looking," I answered and moved on to the back recesses of the closet. All that was back there was my big suitcase. It was partially unzipped at the top. I was certain I'd closed it all the way once I'd unloaded my belongings. My gut told me to check in there, but I didn't want to give Vinnie any ideas. I slid the zipper along the track as quietly as possible and peered inside the case. There was nothing obvious. Certainly, nothing was missing from its depths. But I gave the edges a feel, bumping up against something hard tucked into the lining. It would have been easy to miss if I'd been doing a cursory look. I peeled back the lining to find two small smartphones and Vera's ring.

I guess they didn't find everything they were looking for.

But why would Vera stash this in my bag? Surely she hadn't planned on getting murdered. Was she going to claim I'd stolen it? Either way, there was no chance I was going to let the police take possession of it right away. Not when I could use it to lure whoever had broken in. I turned so my back was to Vinnie before I stashed the ring in my front pocket and tucked the extra phones in my cleavage. Not like Vinnie would be checking there.

"Looks like everything's here," I called to him when I was satisfied I'd secreted the items away.

I left the room and Vinnie stepped in. "You're sure."

"Yeah. I'm a bit of a slob," I replied. I didn't need them trying to dust for fingerprints and finding Vera's on my bag.

I heard footsteps on the stairs, Chief Hayes' voice filling the small corridor. "Vinnie, start processing the first floor once you're done."

"On it, Chief." Vinnie gave me a sympathetic glance. "You'll probably need to stay elsewhere tonight. I don't know how long it's going to take. We have money to put you both up in a hotel. There's one a few miles from town."

"Do you have the money to give us a rental car while you're at it?" Tania asked.

"Afraid not. Displacement funds are limited," Chief Hayes answered.

"Maybe we can crash at Maggie's one more night?" I suggested.

"I'll give her a call."

I retreated outside to wait for Tania to finish going over her room with Chief Hayes. I caught the neighbors to the right poking their heads out of their front doors, checking the cruiser in the drive. They didn't approach to ask why. Ten minutes later, Tania appeared.

"Maggie said it's fine if we go back over and stay at her place tonight." Her tone was all calm and confident.

I gave her an auspicious look. "You're too calm. What's going on?"

"Poor Vinnie may not have noticed the rather rectangular bulge in your bosom, but it doesn't escape me. Also, I'm an empath and you were giving away triumphant vibes all the way out here."

I showed her the two phones and the ring. "Vera had hidden these in the lining of my suitcase. No clue why." And unless we knew someone who could speak to the dead, we would never know.

"Well, if she was traveling with as much money as she gave me, and that ring is as expensive as you think, I'd say she didn't want anyone to find them," Tania posited as we started to make the trek into town and back to Maggie's.

"And she assumed if someone was following her,

they'd look through her things, not mine. Or they'd do a quick look through mine and give up," I added.

"Indeed. Now, the phones are another matter altogether."

"I was certain she had her phone with her when we went to work that morning. But there's definitely two phones," I commented.

"Oh, right. Deputy Ditzy was telling the chief he was surprised Vera didn't have a phone." Sam materialized beside me.

"You are the worst spy ever," I quipped.

That was the second time he'd disparaged poor Vinnie. He couldn't be that much of a ditz. Sam shrugged one translucent shoulder. "I told you, I wasn't paying attention to stuff."

"Look, I'll see if I can figure out anything from the phones while I'm at work tomorrow afternoon." I handed her the ring. "Maybe you can find a safe place to keep this?"

MY PLAN TO STAKE OUT GINNY'S IN THE MORNING WAS thwarted by the magic-infused tea Maggie had shoved into both mine and Tania's hands the moment we'd arrived last night. By the time I woke, it was almost noon and I was due for my partial shift at High Time. When I arrived, I found Sage in the break room.

Sage glanced at me. "Did you manage to clear your head?"

Not at all. "Some. Thanks again for being so lenient. Are we still closing at two today?"

"Through the rest of the week," she answered.

"How's planning going for Vera's memorial gathering on Saturday?"

"Good. We've gotten the town's blessing to hold it on the pier and we're spreading the word. I think we'll have a good turn out."

I had to hope it brought a couple of specific out-of-towners, too. It gave me two days to track down Walter and Vera's fiancé, and figure out what was going on.

"Count me in," I said.

"Great." Sage gave me a relieved smile. "I hate to do this, but do you think you could help out at the register this afternoon?"

"Might benefit from a quick primer on the till first."

"Of course. Thank you." Sage patted my arm and headed toward the kitchen to handle whatever needed her attention back there. I hurriedly opened my locker and stowed the phones at the back behind an extra uniform shirt before heading out to greet the public.

It was quiet for a while and I amused myself with making certain I could operate the till without making a fool of myself. The time ticked over to 1:00 before the bell over the front door signaled my first customer. I'd been so focused on the register that I didn't look up right away.

"Excuse me," a male voice said.

My head whipped up at the intonation. It matched the man who'd argued with Vera three days ago. The same man I suspected was Walter Lawson. He stood there in front of me with dark hair and pale green eyes. I could almost picture his mouth forming the word 'Kenz' when he spoke to Vera three days ago.

Why is he back here?

Surely he knew Vera was dead and not here. Or maybe he didn't? Either way, time to see if he's a cold-blooded killer.

14

In that moment I tried to take in everything about the man in front of me without it being obvious I was studying him. But his hands were in his pockets, and I didn't have the ability to see through fabric to notice if he had tiny cuts or scratches on his hands from the vine. And I couldn't just come round the counter to see if his feet looked to be the right size or check his shoes for mud and grass residue.

"Miss?" his voice pulled me out of my thoughts.

"Sorry," I mumbled and straightened. "Can I help you? Do you have an order to pick up?" I doubted it.

"No, I don't. I was wondering if you could tell me

what sort of products you sell?" He shifted his weight from side to side.

I leaned forward and craned my neck to point at the recently established listing of items. "Everything's up there. It's all cash."

If this was in fact Walter and if my suspicions were right about his identity as the killer and the burglar, he was flush with cash.

"Would you have any recommendations for what would be the most, erm, calming?"

I should know the answer to that. I should be able to tell him which plants were best for easing joint inflammation and pain, and which we cultivated purely for the THC. And yet, I knew none of it. If my magic was functional in any kind of consistent capacity, I might have been able to see if Sage could whip something up for him on the spot.

"I can ask. I'm still pretty new here. I don't know all the formulas," I said.

"Thanks. I'd appreciate that."

"Before I do, I'm going to need to see some ID. Make sure you're over eighteen," I said.

"Oh, right." He pulled a faded brown leather wallet from his pocket and produced a New York driver's license.

He didn't appear to have any marks on his

hands. I took the identification. It confirmed the man in front of me was Walter Lawson. At least that was one less missing piece of this confusing puzzle.

I passed the ID back and he retreated to one of the chairs that lined the waiting area. I could at least see his shoes. I was a terrible judge of foot size, but they looked like they could possibly match the impressions I'd seen. But the shoes didn't look muddy.

I couldn't just stand around gawking at the man. He seemed genuinely interested in making a purchase. So, I locked the register and went to look for Sage. I found her in the office, studying something on the computer. She hit a few keys as soon as I walked in, suggesting it was private content.

"Everything okay?" her pale blue eyes tracked my every move.

"There's a guy out front looking to buy something to help calm his nerves. And I'm embarrassed to admit I've not a clue what to suggest. I thought maybe you'd have some insight."

Sage's brow furrowed and she stood up. "We don't get a lot of walk-ins. Most folks are already regulars by now if they're going to be."

"You must get some folks from out of town

coming here, because it's easier or cheaper than going to other places," I noted.

She shook her head. "Nope. We're a small operation." She led me through the growth room and into the kitchen.

"You said he wanted calming?"

"Yeah. Seems like he could use it." Maybe he was just upset about his sister being dead. Or maybe he had a more nefarious reason to need to make a purchase. I shouldn't jump to conclusions about the man. All I knew for certain was he was looking for his sister and she was dead.

"And you checked his ID to make sure he's legal?"

"Yeah."

"Okay. Do me a favor, go ask if he'd prefer an ointment or edibles. And if it's edibles, ask if he wants baked or gummy."

I gave her a salute and returned to the front of the shop. Walter still sat in the chair, his feet tapping an erratic rhythm as he waited. "Mr. Lawson, do you have a preference on what form it's in?"

"What form?" he replied, confusion coloring his voice.

"Do you want a topical ointment or something edible? We've got cookies or gummies today, I think."

"Oh, right. Uh, gummy I suppose," he answered after giving the sign a quick glance.

I'd been here long enough to memorize the pricing structure. Interesting he'd choose the most expensive option, since he didn't seem to care what he got.

"Just give me a few minutes and I'll be back with your order," I said.

He nodded and I returned to the kitchen to pass along his order to Sage. After conveying it, I watched her go off to chat with one of the confectioners. Thomas bumped my shoulder with his as he rolled out dough.

"How are things at home?" I whispered.

"Better. Thanks," he answered.

"Good. Glad I didn't have to tell Sage she had an unexpected overnight guest."

"So am I."

"Order's up," Sage called and passed me a small bright green bag with the High Time logo stamped on the front.

I brought it out to Walter. He rose and I glanced over his shoulder out the window. I thought I spotted someone across the road, but they disappeared in seconds. I turned my focus back to Walter and said, "That will be forty dollars."

I accepted the two twenty dollar bills he gave me. From what I'd seen, the money Tania had stashed in the vase had been folded rolls of one-hundred-dollar bills. Not that it would take much to change one or two bills into smaller tender.

"Have a good day, Mr. Lawson," I said with a forced smile.

"Thanks." He cast one last glance out the front window before leaving the building.

It still seemed odd he would come back here. I'd missed an opportunity to ask him about what had brought him to town and what was still keeping him here. From our limited interaction, he seemed nice enough. Not the sort of person who would kill his sister. But I also shouldn't judge him from this one interaction.

The last hour of my shift gave me time and privacy to ponder what might be keeping Walter in Brookhaven. A few customers popped by to pick up standing orders. By the time Sage came through and flipped the sign on the front door to 'Closed,' I was ready for a late lunch. I was about to text Tania to ask if she wanted to meet for lunch when I saw a pair of texts from her. One was a photo of a pot of chili. The other was a message reading, **'Lunch at Maggie's.'**

I made the already short trip in half the time, my mouth watering at the thought of Tania's cooking. And my heart did an extra beat at the thought of spending time with Maggie.

"Knock, knock," I announced my presence accompanied by actually rapping my knuckles on the doorframe of Maggie's flat before walking in.

"Food is already on the table," Tania called from the second bedroom.

I sat down at one of the spots and noted only two bowls. Of course, Maggie was still at work. She couldn't just pop home for lunch. Tania appeared, gave me a nod, and sat down across from me.

"I was just stowing our little find somewhere safe. Although, I do think we ought to give it to Rick."

"Is there any chance you could get an empathic hit from it?"

"I'm afraid not. At least not for the killer. I get residual emotions from it that are very clearly Vera. Fear and worry mostly."

I took a bite of chili and savored the rich spices. "Her brother came to the dispensary today."

"He did? Are you sure it was him?"

"I had to verify his ID before I could sell him anything. It was Walter. So, we know he's in town and has been for a few days. His voice is the same as the one I heard talking to Vera."

"What did he want?"

"To buy some product. He seemed pretty agitated and twitchy. It could just be his way of coping with grief over his sister's death or he could be hiding something. I just wish I knew which."

"What is it they say, that killers often return to the scene of the crime?" she noted.

"Yeah, but this felt different. I can't put my finger on it, but he seemed almost nervous. He kept looking out the window. Like he thought someone was watching him." I took another bite. "And it's weird he's still in town."

"He may be waiting for the police to release her body, to take her home to bury her," Tania offered.

"Maybe." I took another bite. "Sage and the rest of the staff are organizing a small service for Saturday. If we can find proof that Walter is the killer, maybe we can lure him out. Make sure Vinnie and Chief Hayes are there to arrest him."

"Don't get ahead of yourself," she chided.

"You're right."

We lapsed into silence as we both ate our meals. Having Tania back on my side was a bigger relief than I'd expected. Thinking it through, I could understand her hesitancy to tell me about the large sum of money she'd come into possession of. I could also get that she was embarrassed by the solvency of the business. I wanted to do something to help her turn around the business, but I was at a loss for what to do.

"I know things have been disrupted with Vera's death, but how has communicating with the plants at the dispensary been going?" Tania broached.

"Poorly. I was making some progress the day Vera died. But since then, there's only been radio silence. Like, even when I'm not trying to get them to react to me, I can still hear them in the back of my mind. They're just waiting for me to listen closely. Except, now I can't even hear that."

"That's odd. Perhaps it's a stress reaction," she said with an unconcerned shrug.

"Is that a thing? Have you ever just lost your magic, because you were stressed? I mean, forgive me for sounding indelicate, but having your business at risk seems like a pretty stressful situation and I don't see you not being able to feel people's emotions."

"I also have three decades more experience with my power than you. When I was first learning to control it, there was a lack of consistency for a time. I can't say for certain that it happened as a result of stress, but magic is a natural part of a person's being. I don't see why it would be any different from stress causing other physiological symptoms."

"Maybe. It just feels strange to not have that connection, especially in a town where it seems like everywhere you turn people have powers. Like, can Tyson teleport or something?"

Tania shook her head. "Tyson had an unfortunate accident where he accepted a cursed object and it blinded him in one eye."

That explained the eye patch.

"He now uses some crystals and a truth spell placed on the shop to gauge his customers better."

"Who put the spell on the place?" I didn't think it was relevant to the problem at hand, but it was fascinating.

Tania snickered. "Ginny of all people."

"I don't believe that. That woman is the epitome of hyperbole."

"While I don't disagree with you on that last point, it is true. Ginny is a fairly powerful witch, when she chooses to use her gifts for good and isn't spending all of her time stirring up controversy all over town."

"Speaking of people all over town, do you think

the break-in has made its way through the gossip mill? I saw our neighbors looking when the police showed up."

Tania made a show of checking the time on the clock over the stove. "By now, yes. I think that cat is out of the bag."

There was very little I could do about that. Time for a different subject. "I managed a look at Walter while he was at the shop today."

"And what did you find?"

"If he was the one who broke in, either he is really good at cleaning his shoes or he brought another pair. And his hands were clean. No cuts or marks like Chief Hayes is looking for."

"Maggie does sell healing products at the clinic. It's entirely possible he went in while she was working before we knew any of that information," Tania offered.

"Chief Hayes had a similar thought about me."

I made a mental note to show Maggie Walter's picture when I saw her next. She might be the key to breaking this whole thing wide open. Before I could think about it more, the alarm on my phone buzzed. I'd set it to remind me to pay Ginny's a visit and see if I could learn anything from her.

"Thanks for lunch. It was fantastic," I said.

"It is nice to have someone around who appreci-ates my cooking."

I stood to leave and she cocked her head to one side. "I thought I saw limited hours at High Time."

"It's closed for the rest of the day, but I've got an errand to run."

If Walter stuck around through Saturday, I doubted he would stay beyond Vera's memorial. Two days felt like a long time and yet I knew it was no time at all. I had to use every avenue available to hunt down the clues.

I made my way toward Ginny's, but stopped when I spotted a man loitering outside of High Time. He kept peering through the front window, even though the sign obviously said 'Closed.' I darted across the street and tapped him on the shoulder.

"It's closed for the day. You'll have to come back tomorrow. We open again at ten," I said.

The man faced me and I reflexively took a step back. He looked eerily like Vera's fiancé from the photos I'd seen. *What is he doing here?* It couldn't be a coincidence that both he and Walter were in town at the same time. Had he been the bearded man I'd seen at Ginny's last week? The one making Vera so nervous.

He pointed to my High Time shirt. "I'm guessing you work here?"

"I do. But like I said, we're closed."

"I've just got a couple questions." He reached into his pocket and pulled out a crisp fifty-dollar bill. "Consider it overtime."

"Any questions would be better directed to the owner," I said, unease washing over me.

"It's nothing too difficult, I promise. I just want to know if this place does a lot of business."

"We do all right. Why?" I didn't want to answer his question and yet I felt almost compelled to reply.

"Well, I heard you all lost an employee suddenly and I might be in the market for a business venture."

"I can ask the owner if she's looking to take resumes."

He shook his head. "You know what, I'm good. I'll come back another time." He pressed the fifty into my palm. "Thanks for your time."

He flashed me a sly grin before heading off down Main Street. I wanted to toss the money. It felt wrong somehow and yet, I found myself pocketing it anyway. I'd been so thrown off by his questions, I hadn't even remembered to look at his hands to see if they bore any cuts, healed or otherwise.

I now knew that Walter and Vera's fiancé were in

town. Had they come looking for her together? Had she been trying to get away from both of them? What motive would either of them really have to want her dead? Had she lied about her identity? She'd clearly done well to keep both her persona as Vera and that of McKenzie separate. Maybe her fiancé had discovered the lie and come to confront her about it before her brother caught up to her. Or maybe they'd both been involved.

I'd thought I had a handle on what might have happened to Vera. Now, all I had was more questions.

My head was spinning by the time I walked into Ginny's. It was quieter than usual, but Ginny still occupied her spot at the middle of the counter. I couldn't just go up to her and ask what she knew about Walter or Vera's fiancé. It would be too obvious and she would see it coming. So, I found an empty table for two and sat down. I would never turn down a cup of coffee and it would let me build the courage to suck up to Ginny.

A redheaded waitress whose name tag read Monica stopped by to offer me water and take my order. She had to go back to the kitchen for a fresh pot of coffee. As I waited for her return, I considered the fact that Ginny, like me, was a witch. Given what Tania had told me about the Hayes family dating back to the Salem Witch Trials, I was surprised Ginny hadn't led with that when we'd first met. Maybe she didn't brag about it to tourists. Her having magic did raise the question of what type of witch she was. If her magic was linked to truth, that would seem to be more of an emotional power, like Tania's. Could I cast spells like she had on Tyson's establishment? Or was that only reserved for certain types of power? I hadn't seen Tania cast any spells. I couldn't say for certain whether what Maggie had done in trying to guide my memories was actual spell work. I was just so new to all of this. And then the realization that she was capable of casting a truth spell sent me into a minor fit of giggles. It seemed so out of character for the woman who shared whatever rumors floated by her with anyone who'd listen.

"I'm so sorry to hear about what happened at Tania's," the gentleman from the library said from the next table over.

I blinked at him, not registering that he was actually talking to me at first. "Thanks. We weren't home." I said.

"Just awful. This town has always been such a safe place. I can't imagine who would want to do something like that," he said, shaking his head.

"I'm sure the police will find the culprit," I offered.

He laughed. "Wouldn't bet money on it. That chief is useless."

"Oh, be quiet, Gerry," Monica said as she came by with a mug and the coffee pot. To me she said, "Don't mind him. He's just bitter he didn't think to run as opposition."

"I still got votes," Gerry protested.

"Because you voted for yourself," Monica sighed with an eye roll. "Let the poor girl drink her coffee in peace."

The commotion had drawn Ginny's attention. Her blonde 'do bounced against her shoulders as she cast her gaze my way. I tried to ignore her and prayed she would at least let me finish one cup of coffee before launching at me. Yes, I wanted to pick her brain, but I intended to do it on my own terms.

Mercifully, she seemed to agree and turned back to her prior conversation. I contented myself with taking slow pulls from my mug. As I drank, I people watched. I hadn't intended to pick a table with a clear view of the front entrance, but here I sat. Aside from Gerry to my left, there was only one other occupied table on this side of the restaurant with a couple of tables filled on the far side. It must just be a slow afternoon. I half expected Walter or Vera's fiancé to materialize, yet the door remained firmly shut.

Slowly, the other patrons began to cycle through. Gerry sat at his table, nursing his own mug of coffee that Monica came by and refreshed twice while I finished mine. She refilled my mug again and I handed over the fifty Vera's fiancé had forced on me and waited for the change. Monica was going to get a generous tip today just so I didn't have to carry the money around. For whatever reason, Gerry seemed intent on staying as long as I sat there.

"Can I ask you something?" I finally said, leaning across the back of the booth seat to address him.

"Sure," he said, setting his cup down.

"I noticed you reading an out-of-date paper earlier. Why is that?"

Gerry chuckled. "I've been out of town a while."

"The paper doesn't have an electronic version?" I noted.

He scoffed. "You, young people and all your computer nonsense. Newspapers are meant to be enjoyed firsthand. The smell of the ink, the texture of the page."

"So, you are what, reading them one by one until you've caught up?"

"Precisely."

"Well, I hope you're able to get current. I'd hate to be perpetually three weeks behind," I said with a laugh.

"I'm a fast reader," he said with a self-important nod.

I laughed and turned away from his seat. The rest of the shop was deserted. It was as good a time as any to grab Ginny's ear. Also, with fewer people around, there would be less chance we'd be overheard. I heard Monica tell the kitchen staff she was going on a smoke break. The door separating the kitchen from the main eating area swung open and shut behind her.

I pushed myself out of the booth and moved to sit beside Ginny, waiting for her to take notice of me. She drummed her nails on the ceramic handle of her oversized coffee mug without looking at me.

"Hi, Ginny," I finally said.

She made a show of turning to look at me, feigning surprise that I now sat beside her. "What brings you over?"

Like you don't already know.

"I wanted to make sure you knew about the service the High Time staff is holding for Vera on Saturday. I'm sure everyone would be grateful to have one of Brookhaven's most prominent families showing their support."

"Sage already asked me and yes, I am going to be there. She didn't need to send you to confirm." Her gaze narrowed. "Then again, I don't really think she did."

She took a slow sip from her mug. "You know, I feel just terrible for Vera. Poor girl, being murdered like that. How awful." She stopped and leaned back. "Then again, I don't have to tell you that."

"I know it's probably none of my business, but you seem to have your finger on the pulse of what's going on in town and you seem to be the first to know when new people come through. Almost like magic. And I had heard your family was prominent for a reason. Something about the Witch Trials?"

I hoped buttering her up, acting as though I was in awe of her talents, would loosen her lips. At the very least it got her attention. She pivoted on her stool to look at me directly.

"There have been Hayes family members in this town since the early seventeen hundreds. Our power and influence have shaped this town. And it is our duty to make sure it stays safe."

"And people come to you, because you know

what's going on," I continued. "Surely, you've got some idea of what's really happening here?"

Her dark gaze narrowed in my direction. "What are you getting at?"

"I know I'm new around here, but I think we both know that I didn't do anything to Vera. No matter what other people have told you. And I certainly didn't break into the B&B. But I'm betting you've got a theory on who did."

She batted her long lashes at me. "I might. But I don't see why I'd share it with you. Especially when you've made my poor brother's life so complicated."

"Stop being a tease, Ginny. Tell the girl what she wants to hear," Gerry called.

"Mind your own business Gerald," Ginny snapped.

I didn't need him butting into the conversation, but if it got her to tell me what she knew about Walter or Vera's fiancé, I'd allow it. Ginny sat there contemplating what she wanted to share with me for a long time. She tapped her hands on the rim of the coffee cup in front of her and took a sip, the contents still high enough to slosh about.

"I think that Vera was leading some sort of double life and it finally caught up to her," Ginny finally offered.

I stared at her in stunned silence. Could we really be of the same mind? It was plausible she'd heard about the second identity from her brother or Vinnie. The latter wasn't exactly careful about leaving evidence in easily accessible locations. But maybe she had spoken to Walter and managed to worm her way into his head and extract information without him noticing.

"Interesting. Wish your brother believed that," I sighed.

"He'll stop hounding you eventually. I just don't think he likes you," she said with a knowing smile. "He's protective of his job and he doesn't need some amateur sleuthing around, messing up his case."

I'm not messing it up!

"I'm not trying to mess anything up. Trouble just seems to follow me," I murmured.

"Some of us are just born unlucky, I suppose," she responded.

"So, let's say for argument's sake that we can agree I didn't do it. Who would you think is a likely suspect? She talked about a brother once or twice," I fibbed. "Seemed not to get on so well with him."

"Well, I don't know about any brother. I didn't really talk to the poor girl much while she was alive. But I may have seen some new faces in town the last week or two besides her. One might have even asked about her."

"What did they want to know?" I pushed.

"A man with that sort of purposely scruffy facial hair look came by asking about her. Honestly, I don't see why people think that's attractive."

That sounded like Vera's fiancé. So, he'd come asking about her. But I was sure I'd heard Walter argue with her the day of her death. Both men had come to High Time after she'd been found, even if Vera's fiancé hadn't gone in. None of this was adding up.

"Did anyone you talk to happen to mention if that guy or anyone else they didn't recognize were lurking about places they weren't meant to be?"

"Isn't that the definition of a stranger? They're somewhere they aren't supposed to be?" Ginny drawled.

She had a point, as irritating as it was. This little interrogation was not going at all like I'd hoped. Sure, she'd confirmed there was more than one new face in town and that Vera's fiancé had specifically asked around about her. But that didn't help me pin down who might have killed Vera.

"Did you happen to notice if the new faces popped up around the same time?" It was entirely possible that Walter found Vera and let her fiancé know and he showed up later.

"Are you looking to form a newbie club or something?" she mocked.

"What? No, I just ... never mind," I answered.

She let out a long huff. "I might have noticed a couple of new guys come in a day or two before the news broke about Vera getting murdered. Mr. Scruffy was one of them." Her tone had an air of irritation, almost like she had unwanted guests lingering in her home.

I knew for a fact neither man had left town yet. And she wasn't happy about their lingering presence. If I could nudge Chief Hayes in the right direction and get both of these men out of town, maybe I could find my way into Ginny's good graces. Then she'd stop spreading rumors that I'd done all manner of criminal acts.

"You may not understand this, but the town has a certain balance to it. And every time someone new traipses in, looking to stay, that balance is disrupted," Ginny said in a clipped tone.

"Well, they have to find their place to fit." I offered.

"Just because you forced yourself in doesn't mean you fit," she snapped.

"I've every right to be here," I replied, my own anger bubbling to the surface. "Just because your brother is the law in this town doesn't make you in charge of the rest of its affairs. No matter your family's history."

She slammed her oversized mug down on the counter, its contents frothing up over the edge as she turned to glower at me. Before she could say more, the front door opened and Monica reappeared, the scent of cigarette smoke trailing in her wake.

Our conversation was over. The waitress fixed both Ginny and I with a questioning stare before she headed back into the kitchen. Ginny's posture shifted and she turned away from me. I had overstayed my welcome.

"Right, well, uh, thanks for the chat," I said and stood up from my stool. The fire that had been burning hot in my belly had died down with the interruption.

"I'd say it was a pleasure, but that would be a lie," Ginny called in a sugary sweet tone as I left the café behind. She really had a bizarre relationship with the concept of truth.

I paused outside the window and caught Gerry's gaze tracking me. I offered up a small wave before I departed. I knew I should head back to Maggie's and regroup with her and Tania. But I needed to clear my head. I did an about face and headed toward the pier. I'd spent more time at Ginny's than I'd expected. It was almost five o'clock and most of the stalls would be closed by now. But empty was what I needed. For the first time since I'd come to Brookhaven, I felt claustrophobic. There were too many people with their watchful gazes and eaves-dropping ears.

I made it to the boardwalk just as the sun touched the horizon line, turning the sky above me to pale shades of pink and purple. It reflected off the water, creating a picturesque image that I could envision some savvy photographer capturing to put on a postcard enticing travelers to come here.

I tried to sort through what I'd learned about Vera and McKenzie. The latter had gone missing after Vera's last posts on Facebook, but before her last Instagram photo with the engagement ring. The timing did seem to coincide with Walter's original missing person's ad in the paper and the website he'd created. So maybe she'd decided she would rather be Vera Chase with the rich fiancé than McKenzie Lawson and she'd taken off.

I still couldn't pin down why Walter would wind up killing her. Unless it had been an accident.

Except the cut vine and the strangulation pointed to planning. He hadn't just come onto Tania's property, clipped a length of vine, and brought it with him unless he planned to use it. But there was another option. Maybe Vera's fiancé was mad she'd run off with that ring and he'd been the one to kill her.

Almost on cue, I heard the wooden boards of the pier groan under another person's weight. I pivoted to see the silhouette of a man standing a few feet away. He turned long enough for me to verify it was Walter before he startled like a deer caught in traffic and bolted.

Interesting. Had he come here to think, too? This was the second time I'd seen him here. I started after him, but lost him before I'd made it past the spot where Maggie and I had shared lunch. No one should be able to move that fast. Not naturally anyway. Could he have some sort of supernatural ability, too?

Vera had been almost offended when she'd discovered me attempting magic. If her own brother had abilities, surely it wouldn't have led to such a reaction. Unless his power is what drove her away. Given my own experience, that was a real possibility. I was still no closer to unraveling this mystery and it frustrated me.

But maybe I had an avenue open to me that I wasn't seeing. If Walter had come here twice, perhaps he would again. I could stake out the pier early in the morning. If he was looking for other ways to calm himself, seeing a beautiful sunrise without other people around was one way to do it.

As I wound my way back to Maggie's, I resolved to be up before the sun in the morning and track Walter down. I was going to get him to tell me what he was still doing in town. If I was lucky, I might just land a confession.

16

I'm not normally a morning person, yet I was up even before my phone buzzed at me to get out of bed at five o'clock. I did my best to pull on clothes and a light jacket—being near the water was still chilly even in the summertime—and crept past Maggie snoring softly on the couch. I spotted Beau lounging on the back of the furniture.

"Oy, come along you. I need your help today," I whispered and held out an arm for him.

He blinked twice at me before crawling along the back of the couch and up my arm. He nestled against my neck and the familiar weight of him buoyed me as I went in search of a potential killer and thief. Main Street was appropriately deserted at this hour. Most businesses didn't open until eight or nine and their owners didn't live far from them. There was no need for them to be up now.

"You know, I was kind of annoyed you weren't home during the break-in, but now that I've had time to think about it, I'm glad you weren't. You could have gotten hurt," I told the reptile.

'Camouflage.'

There was a hint of derision in the word as it echoed in my head. As if he wanted to add 'you stupid woman,' but hadn't quite managed it. "I know you can hide, but still. Not even you're impervious."

I took a leisurely pace to the pier, hoping my hunch that Walter would be there panned out. As I walked, I took in the beauty of the place I now called home. If I'd gone out at this hour in the city, there would have already been hundreds of people clogging up the streets, rushing to the tube for work or coming home off a night shift. There would have been noise and pollution. I'd been raised in that environment and yet it hadn't struck me til I'd come here that the slower pace of small town life was really more my speed.

I reached the pier and at first glance it was deserted, just like the rest of the main thoroughfare. I could wait. Although if I'd been smart I would have packed a thermos of coffee to keep me company.

Unfortunately, there weren't any retail chains in town and even Ginny's, while doing earlier hours than most businesses, was not open yet, either.

"You're interrupting my 'me time,'" Sam's voice came to me on the breeze.

"Didn't come looking for you," I told him as he materialized beside me. "I'm looking for someone else."

He arched a brow at me, and I took in his skintight outfit. It wasn't one I'd seen before and was devoid of most of the bright colors and sparkles he was prone to. I really ought to ask him how he managed to change outfits when he was a ghost. Though now was not the time to indulge my curiosity. "Well, I know you're not out here looking for Maggie. Not even the dead could wake her at this hour."

"Tried it, have you?" I quipped.

"Maybe." He flashed a cheeky grin. "So, if you're not here looking for the town's eligible healer, then who are you looking for?"

"Vera's killer. Or at least her brother, who I'm hoping can shed some light on what happened to her."

"Oh honey, trust me being dead isn't all it's cracked up to be. And I've kind of got the whole house haunting down to a science. I don't need you messing up my mojo."

I waved off his sass. "Relax, I'm not planning on getting myself murdered. Anyway, like I said, I'm really just hoping Walter can tell me why he's stuck around town and give me any hint about what really happened to Vera."

"And you're here because ...?" Sam trailed off.

"I saw him here last night and earlier in the day. For some reason he seems to like the pier, so I was hoping he'd show up again."

"I haven't noticed anyone today. What's he look like?"

I took out my phone and pulled up one of the photos on McKenzie's page. Sam leaned in close. "Hmm, now that I think about it, I have seen him. He's come down here in the morning the last couple days."

"Great. Where have you seen him exactly?"

"You really think confronting him is a good idea?"

"I told you, I just want to talk to him. I'm not going to flat out accuse him of anything. But there's something that feels off about this whole thing and if I don't figure it out, it's going to drive me mad." I stowed my phone. "Now, tell me where you've seen him."

Sam pointed to the far end of the boardwalk. Maybe Sam had distracted me or maybe Walter had some sort of teleportation magic after all, because I could swear I hadn't seen him standing there a moment ago. Yet, a male figure stood staring out at the horizon line. Daybreak was just beginning to color the sky in vibrant shades of orange, as if burning the darkness of night away. It really was beautiful. I could see why Sam liked to come out here so much. I closed the distance and upon closer inspection, confirmed it was indeed Walter.

I inched closer, my foot landing on a squeaky board. Walter's head whipped around and he visibly shrunk away from me. Guess those pot gummies weren't doing anything to calm his nerves now.

"Sorry, I didn't mean to disturb you," I said, holding my hands up in a placating gesture.

"You're the girl from the dispensary," he said.

"That's me. Darcy," I replied and took another step or two closer. He glanced my way and I could tell that his eyes were a little glassy. He was high, which could work to my advantage.

"What are you doing here?"

"Just out for a walk. I find it's peaceful out this

time of day," I said, coming to stand beside him. "How about you?"

"It was her favorite time of day and she loved the water," he murmured.

"Whose?"

"What?" He seemed to catch himself before he added, "Sorry, I mean it's my favorite."

No, you didn't.

"You aren't from around here," I said.

"What gave it away?"

"The New York address on your license," I replied.

"Oh. Yeah, I guess that would do it."

"I've seen you around town for a few days, but I know for a fact there's only one lodging house in town. Where have you been staying?"

If he was put off by my direct questioning, he didn't show it. "There's a hotel a couple miles outside of town, on the highway."

Probably the same one Vinnie and Chief Hayes had offered to foot the bill for Tania and I after the break-in. Could it be where Vera's fiancé was holed up, too?

"Did you know her?" His question felt like a non sequitur, but it gave me an in to talking about Vera. Or McKenzie as he knew her.

"You mean Vera, the girl who was killed? Not too well. She'd only been around a week or so. But we were both staying at the B&B."

Tears welled in the man's eyes. "I haven't been able to get her out of my head," he admitted.

"Me either," I said, leaning into it. "But I mean, you've got no reason to worry about her. It's not like you knew her."

"I thought I did," he sighed.

"You met her before she died?" I knew he had.

"I've known her all of her life," he said. The marijuana was making his lips loosen.

"Oh. You were good friends then?"

He gave a sad laugh. "No, she's my sister. She wasn't exactly proud of our family. I miss her."

"Well, surely you've spoken to the police, then. Let them know there's someone to claim her."

"I ..." he trailed off into silence.

Why wouldn't he go to the police? Was he afraid to face what he'd done? Or was it just too much for his psyche to actually see his dead sister's body? I let the question drop.

"Well, I'm still very sorry for your loss. There's going to be a memorial on Saturday. Will you be staying to attend?"

"They're honoring a version of her I never knew.

It would be like walking into some stranger's funeral," he said.

"What makes you say that?"

"I don't know a Vera. I know McKenzie. And she wouldn't lie about who she was, no matter what she was going through."

I wanted to ask what he meant by lying, but his interaction at High Time came to mind. "Before she left New York, did she ever mention a boyfriend? Or someone serious like that?"

"No. But in all honesty, the last few months before she took off, we weren't really talking much. If she was seeing someone, it's news to me." He swallowed. "It's going to sound strange, but I can't shake the feeling that she's still out there. I know she's laying in a morgue, but it's like, I don't know, maybe her spirit is lingering?"

"I've heard weirder things," I answered and glanced in Sam's direction. He remained invisible to Walter's eyes. "Maybe getting her belongings back would give you some sense of closure?"

"Maybe."

"I'm sure once the police are done with their investigation, they'd be happy to release them to you. Was there anything you were hoping to get back?" A ring perhaps.

"She had some jewelry that I think our mother would like to have back."

Not what I'd expected to hear, but it could encompass a fancy engagement ring. I didn't know their family dynamic. That was the way I would lure him in. Offer up the ring and see if he showed up. Then I could force him to admit the truth.

"I hope you get it back," I said, sensing it was time to make my exit.

"I just wish I knew why she told me she didn't recognize me," he sighed.

I stopped mid-motion. "Maybe she was just surprised to see you."

"No. It was like she didn't even know me ..." He trailed off into silence again.

I took a few steps backward, letting him fall back into his own head. He'd admitted he'd seen Vera at least once. I still hadn't asked Sage about that video footage. Now seemed like as good a time as any to sort that out. It was curious he didn't know about her fiancé, though. Maybe she'd created the Vera persona to hide the relationship? I still didn't have a clear motive for why Walter would be the one to kill her.

I left Walter to watch the rest of the sunrise in peace as I swung by Ginny's and got a muffin to go, arriving just before 9:15 at High Time. The back door was locked when I arrived, but I pulled the spare key from its hiding spot and let myself in. I didn't expect to find anyone else in the building, especially since Thomas had confirmed he'd patched things up at home, but I walked into the employee area to find Sage standing there.

"Hi boss," I greeted. Maybe it was the universe's way of saying I was on the right track, putting us both here so early.

"Oh, hi, Darcy. I didn't hear you come in. I thought I'd locked the back door."

I headed for my locker as I said, "You did."

"Oh."

"What are you doing here this early? I thought everything was prepped last night for when Thomas and the others come in," I noted.

"I posted Vera's job online and I've been getting a bunch of applications. Vetting them is taking longer than I'd like."

"Oh? I didn't think the process was so complicated," I noted.

"Yeah, well, it turns out I didn't do such a great job with Vera. Chief Hayes came by asking questions about a name I didn't recognize, attached to Vera's picture."

"Oh, how weird."

"So, now I'm taking extra precautions."

"Speaking of weird things, I'd heard her argue with a customer not long before she died. I told all of this to Chief Hayes and reminded him you'd probably have video footage. Did he ever ask about that?"

Sage let out an exasperated sigh. "I knew I was forgetting to do something." She rubbed at her forehead. "Might explain the two missed calls from Vinnie last night."

"Why don't you just go do it now?" I suggested, silently hoping she wouldn't mind if I tagged along.

"I probably better do that. Do you mind coming with me? You would know the timeframe better than I would."

Part of me wanted to tell her she should just give them all of the footage for that day, but I wasn't going to argue about getting a chance to see Walter's confrontation with Vera.

"Of course. Anything I can do to help." After a beat, I added, "Are there any cameras in the grow room?"

"No, although maybe there ought to be with everything that's been happening lately," Sage answered.

I shut the door to the locker and followed her

back into the office. I peered at the computer screen as she tapped away, bringing up two different camera angles. She found the files from four days ago and brought them up, turning to look at me.

"When was it again?"

"Oh, uh, around ten or eleven."

She fast forwarded at 1.5x speed until she hit 10:00. She hit play and I watched as a few people came in and out. Then, I spotted Walter walking up the street. I didn't think he realized he'd been caught on camera as he walked inside. On the interior camera I could see him step up to the counter and engage with Vera. Her face visibly darkened as he spoke to her. I could see him reach a hand across the counter to touch her, but she pulled away.

He lingered for a moment before turning and leaving again. It hadn't been a long exchange, but it was enough to give Chief Hayes a real reason to track him down. Especially as the video played on, revealing me taking over and then Vera stepping outside the dispensary a short while later. Other passersby milled around on the periphery of the camera's range. They were mostly blurry silhouettes and people in profile. They likely hadn't even realized what they'd seen.

I leaned in closer, watching as she started down

the street. Tania intercepted her just within frame and they stood on the sidewalk talking for a few minutes before Vera vanished from sight. Tania disappeared in a different direction about thirty seconds later. I studied the video and spotted Walter walking after Vera about half a block back. He'd gone after her again. I thought I spotted a phone in his hand, before he too, vanished from the camera's view. Did he find a way to track her? Is that how he had ended up here in Brookhaven? The messages he'd gotten on his website had been vague on location. Just the right state. The clip ended as a few other people crossed the street. I thought I caught a bearded man move through the frame, strolling at a leisurely pace, hands in his pockets. Could that be Vera's fiancé?

Bugger, the phones!

I'd completely forgotten the phones stashed in my locker. I'd been so focused on trying to follow other leads, I'd completely ignored the most obvious ones in front of me.

"It looks like he was following her when she left," I finally said as Sage saved the clip and forwarded it to the police.

"Certainly did. Not sure what they talked about, but I don't think he was trying to apologize."

No, I suspected he was trying to get her to come home.

"But it's out of my hands now. The police will do whatever it is they need to do to track him down and get a statement." She logged out of the surveillance program and locked the computer again. "Now Vinnie should stop hounding me. I need to get ready to open. I'll stop by the grow room later and see how things are going."

Maybe Walter would be forthcoming with the police. The lack of injuries to his hands suggested he wasn't involved, but as Chief Hayes had noted, Maggie could work some serious magic. I needed to touch base with her on whether she'd sold him or anyone else balms for their hands. Also, I needed to get my hands on that vine, or even just a piece of it. My magic might have been on the fritz the last few days, but I could make it work again. I could push through stress if it meant making sure the police got the right killer. I still felt so far away from real answers and this might point me in the right direction. I just needed a little more time and a lot of luck.

17

Making it through the morning was agony. I considered calling Maggie just to ask her my questions, but I didn't actually have her number and I couldn't leave Sage short-handed. Still, being around the plants had given me a chance to see if I could work through the stress-induced blockage as Tania had dubbed it.

I started with the more mature plants. They didn't need as much coaxing so it shouldn't have been a big deal to get them to grow. I sat beneath one of the halogen lights and pressed my fingertips to the stem of the smallest of the plants. It was still larger than the seedling I'd been working on earlier in the week.

"I know things have been wonky lately, but I

really need to know I can do this. So, if you could just grow a little, I'd really appreciate it," I told the plant.

Shutting my eyes, I took slow, steady breaths and tried to feel the magic that ran through the world. I let myself focus on the way the stem felt against my skin. I imagined the pulsing energy and life force of the plant as it took nutrients from its roots, funneled them up through the stem and into the leaves.

Not even a tremor against my fingers to signal it was trying to respond. I let go and tried a different plant, one that needed to grow more. I even tried to help it stand taller and spread its leaves toward the lights above as I willed it to grow. Still nothing.

The tiny seedling at the end of the tray remained stubbornly hidden in its soil. If anything, it had sunk back below the surface entirely. I pressed the pads of my thumbs into the dirt where the tiny shoot had been and whispered, "Come on now. You want to grow. You know how."

By the time lunch rolled around, I sat with my head in my arms, trying desperately not to weep in frustration. No matter how many plants I'd tried, they all remained painfully silent. I had spent so long trying to push my gift away rather than embrace it. Now that it had deserted me, I didn't feel like myself anymore.

"Hey, Sage needs you up front," Thomas' voice startled me and I gripped the table to avoid falling flat on the floor.

"Why?"

"She just said to send you out," he replied and retreated to the kitchen.

Every step of the short walk to the front of the shop made my dread and panic ratchet higher, tightening my chest until it hurt to breathe. I pushed my way through the dividing door to find Maggie standing there. All of the worry melted away and I gave an audible sigh of relief.

"Sorry to disturb you at work, but I needed to borrow you," Maggie said, giving Sage an apologetic look.

"It's break time anyway. Just clock out first," Sage said.

I darted back through the grow room and into the break room long enough to clock out before returning to the front of the shop. I followed after Maggie, letting her lead me wherever she wanted to go. I did pay more attention to the little camera sitting above the door as we exited, taking in the radius of its field.

"So, did you really need to borrow me?" I asked, falling into step beside her as she led me to the clinic.

Perfect, I can ask her about Walter.

"Well, sort of. Tania mentioned you were having some trouble with your magic being blocked and I thought I might be able to help. I know the spell to recover your memory wasn't a rousing success. But I'm starting to think that's because there was nothing to recover."

"I think you're right. Anything you can do to help would be great. I have a lead I need to follow, but I need my magic to do it," I admitted as she brought me through the aisles to a small office with a single exam bed.

"What are you getting into?" she probed, shutting the door behind her.

I hadn't actually figured out a plan yet. I knew I needed to get my hands on the vine used to strangle Vera. But it was tightly locked up in evidence at the station and I had no business going down there while Chief Hayes and Vinnie were around.

"I hadn't gotten that far, yet."

"Well, whatever you're cooking up, you better not be going alone."

"I'll try," I said as she sat in front of me on a three-legged stool and took my hands in hers.

"Sam told me you went looking for her brother this morning."

"For someone who is dead, he has a surprisingly big mouth. Could give Ginny a run for her money," I scoffed. After a moment, I added, "And all I did was talk to Walter. Not that I learned anything useful."

"Right."

"You didn't see him come into the clinic by chance after Vera's death, did you? Or her fiancé? Maybe to get some healing balm to treat some cuts from vine prickers?" I pulled out my phone and flipped through, showing her photos of each man in turn.

Maggie shook her head. "I've only had a few people in this week for actual medical attention and I don't remember seeing anyone with scratches."

"Well, it was worth a shot."

"Although now that you mention it, I did see that a bottle of ointment was missing. I figured I must have miscounted, but I suppose someone could have stolen it."

I hadn't had reason to take a good look around the pharmacy area of the clinic so I couldn't say whether her wares were detailed in their labeling. But knowing Maggie, they would be.

"Have you got cameras?"

"I don't. Most people know to just ask me for things. I'm usually pretty open to getting them what they need, even if they can't pay for it."

"Right. Small towns being so trusting and all," I muttered.

"Look, how about we focus on you here for a minute?" She prompted.

I cleared my throat. "Yeah, of course. Only have so much time before I've got to get back."

Her firm hands gripped mine as she took a deep breath. I could feel her skin warm against mine and a sense of peace washed over me. I didn't know how her magic worked exactly, but if this was what it always felt like, I should be seeing her for regular sessions.

"Okay, this is going to sound a bit silly, but I need you to go with me on it. I need you to picture your magic in your head."

"Erm, what?"

"Picture it. Whatever it looks like to you when you use it."

"I've never thought about it. It's still so new."

"Well, now's a great time to start. Because if you

aren't in tune with your magic and know what it looks and feels like, you're not going to have a very good relationship with it."

I let out a hiccup of nervous laughter. "You act like it's a living thing."

"Magic is a part of us and the world. So, in a sense, it is a living thing," she countered. "Now, close your eyes and tell me what you see."

Maybe it was the reassuring touch of her hands in mine, but I tried to relax into it and closed my eyes. At first, nothing happened. The space behind my eyelids was blank and dark. But then, slowly, a little seed materialized. It sprouted tiny roots, as if to connect itself to me.

That seems about right.

"I see it. It's a little seedling. Not very big. No leaves or anything. More like a bulb I suppose," I said.

"Is there anything that is keeping it from blooming?"

I wanted to shake my head that there wasn't, but I suddenly found it difficult to breathe. The little seedling in my mind was trying to grow leaves and sprout flowers. Only it was like there was no air to help it on its way.

"No air," I gasped.

"Okay. Something is blocking your access. I need you to take deep breaths for me."

I tried, but my chest only tightened with each shallow breath I took. Maggie's hands tightened around mine and the tingling sensation of her magic zipped up my arms like an electrical current, settling in my breastbone. It eased the constricting feeling.

"Did I do this?" I rasped. "Did I do this to my magic?"

"I don't think it was intentional. And I'm sure it's reversible. When exactly did you notice you'd lost your connection?"

"After Vera's death. When Chief Hayes was asking me questions about plants."

"Stress can absolutely affect a person's magic. Had you been using your power before it happened?"

I nodded. "It's what Vera and I argued about before she left the dispensary. She caught me trying to coax a seedling to grow."

"But you haven't been able to use it since."

"Maybe I let Chief Hayes get in my head. He seemed oddly convinced I was lying about that memory gap. But he took my blood to test for drugs. Maybe that worry shut the magic out?"

Maggie sighed and pulled her hands away.

"That is possible. Fears, whether voiced or not, can have a profound effect on a person's connection to magic."

"Yeah, but what if the magic somehow got away from me and I did something that I don't remember?"

"Has it ever led you to harm another person?"

"Well, no."

"And have you ever wanted to use it to harm someone?"

"No. Of course not!"

"Then what makes you think that would suddenly change just because someone saw you practicing your craft in a town full of magic?"

I wanted to give her an answer, but no good one came to mind. She was right. Getting caught out by Vera wouldn't change me as a person or make me violent. Which meant it was entirely possible the same was true of Walter or her fiancé.

"So, how do I fix this?"

"You need to nurture that seed within you. Give it room and air to breathe and grow. Don't hold it back."

"That all sounds great in theory, but how do I actually do that?"

"You need to trust yourself. I can't tell you what

that looks like. It's something you'll have to figure out on your own."

That was less than helpful. I did my best to mask the disappointment on my face as she let me up and I headed back to High Time. I now had to figure out a way to fix my magic and get my hands on the vine that currently still sat in evidence.

'Beau, if you can hear me, I need you and Sam to meet me at High Time after closing.'

I wasn't going to risk putting Maggie or Tania in the line of fire, but a little breaking and entering seemed right up Sam's alley.

REALIZING IT WOULDN'T DO TO WALK IN DURING BROAD daylight, I'd returned to the library to wait out the afternoon. I spotted Gerry in his armchair. By the date on the paper he had clutched in his hands, he'd made it three days farther in his quest to get caught up. When my phone read 5:07 p.m., I decided I'd waited long enough. I walked to within a block of High Time as that's where I'd told Beau to meet me, but I was beginning to think Beau hadn't gotten my message. I had no way of knowing how far of a range he had and if he was attuned just to me or anyone of his choosing.

"So, why are we meeting in secret?" Sam called as he materialized around the corner.

"Because we're going to do something very illegal and I didn't want anyone else to know," I answered.

Sam flashed me a toothy grin. "I knew you were naughty. What did you have in mind?"

"I need to get into the police station and get my hands on some evidence. But I can't be seen and no one can know I was there."

"You came to the right ghost," he said.

'Dangerous,' Beau added, lumbering up to my feet.

"That's why I've got you both with me," I said, looking down at the chameleon.

"What are we waiting for?" Sam said. If his feet had been touching the ground, he would have been bouncing excitedly on the balls of his feet. As it was, he sort of bobbed up and down.

"Well, I don't want to risk running into Vinnie or Chief Hayes, but they both basically work all the time."

"They brought in a temp to cover the phones in the evenings. He's a real bore," Sam informed me.

"I'd prefer not to encounter anyone alive."

Sam snickered. "I'm pretty sure he barely counts."

"Fine. But we better not get caught," I sighed and started for the station.

We stopped half a block away and I waited for Beau to get comfortable around my shoulders and extend his camouflage to me. I went around to the back of the station toward the impound lot and prayed the surveillance camera didn't pick up the door opening and closing of its own accord.

I held my breath as I crept down the back hallway that dead ended at a single holding cell that sat empty. It gave me a view of the front of the station where indeed a bored looking man with close cropped brown hair sat at the only other desk in the place. His head lolled to one side and I almost waved Sam onward to make sure he was asleep when another chair squeaked. I stopped mid-step to see Vinnie pivoting in his chair. He turned in my direction and I caught the bleary look in his eyes from not sleeping much. The sound of his chair roused the other man who startled awake with a snort.

So much for the easy way. They were both distracted, but there was no guarantee that would last. I turned in a slow circle, not spotting anything that looked like evidence lock-up. Sensing my confusion, Sam pointed to the hall that led to the interview room. I tiptoed down the corridor to a door that was marked with the world's smallest sign reading, 'Evidence.' They must not want the general public to know where they kept their confiscated goods.

Tugging the hem of my shirt up over my hand again, I turned the handle, letting the door swing inward on its hinges. Lights on a sensor flipped on overhead when I stepped in. It was no bigger than a closet. In fact, it had probably been built for that purpose once upon a time. There also wasn't much in terms of evidence sitting on the shelves. There was a box to my left marked 'Active' that held Vera's wallet, the extra ID bearing McKenzie's name, and the length of vine. I half expected there to be something from the break-in, but the thief had been careful not to leave anything behind.

"And here I thought I wouldn't find it," I murmured.

"Uh, you do know that if you take the whole thing they're going to notice. Chief Hayes isn't stupid," Sam hissed in my ear.

"I'm not going to take all of it," I answered as I plucked the bag from the box.

I did my best to get the vine uncoiled within the

confines of the bag. I spotted some dark staining on one portion near one of the ends. My stomach lurched at the realization it was probably blood. If I was lucky, it would be from the killer.

I needed to take just a piece of it, but there was nothing obvious I could use to cut it. My hands trembled as I cast about, looking for anything I could use. I should have come prepared. Beau's claws dug into my shoulder and I winced.

"What was that for?" I whispered, fighting the urge to reach up and rub the sore spot.

"I think he's offering you an option," Sam drawled.

"What, is he gonna nibble his way through it?" I joked.

'Hurry.'

"This is mad," I huffed as I opened the evidence bag. There was no way I was going to touch the vine with my bare hands while it was still in police custody. Out of the corner of my eye, I spotted a box of gloves and tugged two loose. Beau leaned down and with an impressive chomp, the bit of vine with the blood on it fell into my hand.

Chameleons didn't have that sharp of a bite. Then again, chameleons generally weren't telepathic. Chalk it up to another oddity of my magical reptilian friend. I grabbed a spare evidence bag and slid the pilfered vine into it before sealing up the first bag and stashing it in the 'Active' box again.

"Let's go." I eased the door to the evidence closet shut and crept back toward the back door.

"I cannot believe we pulled that off," Sam said with excitement once we were safely on our way to Maggie's.

"Now we just have to hope it was worth it."

18

wanted to spring into action, to see if I could get the piece of vine to lead me straight to the killer. But I hadn't broken through the blockage Maggie identified and my magic had to cooperate in order to get me where I needed to be. I required help. Guidance.

"Do you have any idea how dangerous and reckless that was?" Tania chided, raising her voice at me for the first time since I'd known her.

It felt like she was scolding a rebellious teenager. I suppose she wasn't wrong. I'd been so focused on getting the evidence, I hadn't thought about the risks. Not fully. This town was full of magic and other people with powers. There was no guarantee

Beau's ability to blend in would have hidden me from everyone.

"Well, I can't change it now. I've got the vine and I need to make it work. Please, I need your help?" I begged.

"I should have known you'd try something like this," Maggie added.

I looked at her. "You told me not to do it alone. I wasn't alone. I had Beau and Sam with me."

"That's not what I meant," Maggie railed, throwing her hands up in the air. "I meant people with heartbeats. And I certainly wouldn't have encouraged you if I knew you'd planned on stealing evidence."

I let out an aggravated sigh. "I get what I did was stupid, but it's done now, so can you please help me track down a killer?" I glanced at Tania. "If I'm right and the same person broke in here, we'd be catching a thief, too."

The wrinkles around her eyes looked more pronounced as she rubbed at her face. She was tired and this whole ordeal was weighing on her more than I'd realized. She'd seemed not to let anything faze her when we'd first met. I wasn't used to seeing this vulnerable side to her. "Of course, I want that," she finally answered.

Maggie sat down across from us and raked her fingers through her short hair. "Okay, what exactly are you hoping to do?"

"I'm hoping it can show me where to find the killer," I explained.

"And who do you think that is?" Maggie prodded.

"I don't know. I mean, when I talked to Walter, he seemed like a lost soul. Not someone who'd just committed felonies. And I got a weird vibe when I ran into Vera's fiancé at High Time the other day after closing. But I have nothing leading me to think he'd do anything. I don't even know that they crossed paths. I do know that Walter had a bad interaction with her the day she was killed."

"You found Walter once already," Tania pointed out.

"I didn't have anything to link him definitively to the crime." I pulled the small bit of vine from my pocket. "But there has to be a way to let this lead me to the right person." I turned to face Tania. "Like that leaf left behind in the hit and run. That led me to the culprit. This should do the same, right?"

"Honestly, I don't know. You were following the plant. But I suspect this, if it were even alive, would lead you back to where you took it from."

That was a problem. The vine was very much dead. At least, I was mostly sure it was dead. "Yeah, but that leaf last time had been discarded. It wasn't much more living than this. I think it's just been quiet, because my magic is so out of whack."

"Then you better work on unblocking your connection. Remember, you need to let the seed breathe and grow," Maggie reminded me.

Easier said than done.

But I had no choice. I needed my magic to lead me to the killer and not back to Vera's body in the morgue. "Okay. I can do that. I think," I said, addressing Maggie.

"The couch might be more comfortable," she offered and I moved from the small kitchen table to the couch.

I closed my eyes and envisioned that small bulb of my magic. Immediately, the stifling lack of air hit me and my hands flew to my chest, clawing at it in a feeble effort to force air into my lungs.

"What is going on?" Tania asked, her voice inching up in her vocal register.

"Darcy, I know it feels like you can't breathe right now, but you can. You are the one in control. You just have to tell your body to do it," Maggie coached.

I tried to take her words to heart, but she was

wrong. I wasn't in control of my body. My lungs refused to expand, and I could see the magical bulb within me starting to wither from being starved of what it needed.

'Breathe.' Beau's voice rang out in my mind and I felt his presence curl up on my chest. I clutched at him for reassurance. *'Embrace your power.'*

I could do this. Magic was part of me, and I shouldn't be afraid of it or embarrassed by it. I'd come here looking to nurture it, learn to harness it, and let it grow.

Moment by moment the oppressive lack of air lessened and I could inhale again. The bulb in my mind's eye straightened and tiny green shoots poked forth from the stem. I even spotted a few tiny petals starting to unfurl at its heart in soft orange hues.

I opened my eyes to find Tania and Maggie both standing over me. Beau still sat on my chest, and I wanted to cling to him for dear life. I couldn't explain why, but I knew that without him the connection would have died on the vine.

"I think it worked," I said and sat up, dislodging Beau from his perch.

"Give it a try," Tania said and passed me the evidence bag.

I took a steadying breath as I reached in and

pulled out the vine. I needed to know that the plant could still communicate with me before I could even think about trying to follow the blood trail.

I cradled the vine in my hands and focused all of my attention on it. The living room and my companions vanished until the plant matter and I were the only things that existed. I strained my ears to hear its call and ever so faintly a buzzing reached my ears.

"I've got something," I announced. "It's faint. I'm not sure if it's going to be enough."

I felt a warm hand cradle mine and the soothing touch of Maggie's healing magic boosted my signal. The vine grew warm in my hand and that strange tug I felt the last time I'd let my magic lead me to the answer took over.

THE SUN HAD ALREADY SET WHEN I REACHED THE street. Businesses up and down Main Street and Center Street were beginning to shut their doors for the night. Some would open again tomorrow for weekend hours, while others remained shut until Monday. It meant I had the streets to myself and I could wander without having to worry too much about people noticing me.

"Okay, let's find our killer."

I kept my hand wrapped tight around the vine in my pocket. Somehow the thorns didn't break my skin. Maybe I have more control over my magic than I realized. The surface warmed in my hand and tugged me along and I followed its almost magnetic pull, not paying attention at first to where it led me. By the time I realized where it was leading me, I was already standing in front of the police station.

"Pretty sure he's not there," I muttered under my breath. Not unless Vinnie or the temp were hiding some seriously twisted personalities. In all likelihood, the vine was trying to reunite with the piece from which it had come. That didn't help me.

I forced my feet to move down the street and tried to give the vine more direction. "I need to find the person who used you."

I just hoped it didn't try to take me back to Beau or worse yet, just stand still. Thankfully, it seemed to intuit my request and led me off again. Unfortunately, it pointed me at the B&B where it had been severed from the rest of the plant.

"Maybe there's just too much damage that's been done to you," I sighed.

By now, Vinnie and Chief Hayes had done all they were going to do both inside and out of the

B&B. I expected them to call Tania and let her know we could return to the premises if we felt comfortable. So being on the property didn't bring with it the same illicit feeling as when I'd snuck in last.

I walked down the length of the fence and crouched at the vines twisting over the vinyl façade. The piece of vine in my pocket hummed, sensing it had reunited with its point of origin.

I still didn't quite understand how my magic worked let alone how I could tell what the plant needed or was feeling, but I knew deep in my core that the vine needed that connection with the part that had been severed. So, I tugged it loose from my pocket pressing the two ends together.

I had no idea what I expected to happen when they touched. But the ends sparked as if they were live wires and the bit I'd stolen from evidence brightened and the buzzing in my head grew louder. *Did I just rejuvenate it?*

Whatever I'd managed, the pilfered piece of vine grew hot in my fingers and practically leapt out of my hand. It pulled me onward like a dog seeking a scent. I went back the way I'd come, past the station and out toward the edge of town and the highway. Finally, I stopped outside Tyson's Treasures.

I didn't dare go in, knowing now that it was

protected by a truth charm. I wasn't about to admit my crime to Tyson. And I somehow doubted that he would be harboring either Walter or Vera's fiancé. Unless one or both of them had come in looking to use some of the stolen money or ask if Vera had pawned the engagement ring. I could see through the shop's front window, but didn't spy anyone standing on the customer side of the counter. I doubted Tyson let random strangers into the heart of his shop, which meant whoever the vine was following wasn't here anymore. *Not helpful.*

"Maybe I need to be more specific?" I wondered aloud before looking down at the vine writhing between my fingers. "I need to find where the person who used you is now, not where they've been."

The vine trembled against the palm of my hand, growing warmer by the second and I feared it would ignite. I pressed it between my hands hoping to cool it down and avoid getting burned should it decide to combust when it started undulating toward the highway.

"Okay. If you're sure," I muttered and let the vine hover a few inches above my hand.

The very edge of town was devoid of much save for Tyson's and a gas station that only had one pump. The vine led me along the side of the highway for a short distance before stopping. That seemed odd, but as I looked around, I noted a small barren patch of dirt where cars could pull off in case of emergency. I spotted tire marks in the dirt, as if someone had driven away in a hurry. Had Walter finally gone to claim Vera's body and gotten scared off? Or was her fiancé in a rush to get back to New York for some reason? Either way, if they'd passed beyond Brookhaven's borders, I had no business following them. I didn't have a car—the police still hadn't released Tania's back to her, and I had no sense of where I'd end up. Besides, I wasn't going anywhere alone in the dark. That was just asking for trouble I didn't need.

I stowed the bit of vine back in my pocket and retreated to the center of town. The sun had fully set by now and the streetlamps with their round bulbs and hazy lights lit the walk back to Maggie's flat. As I reached the door, I couldn't shake the feeling of being watched again. I turned and thought I spotted a male shaped shadow dart out of view. It could have been anyone; Walter or Vera's fiancé. Or even Vinnie or Chief Hayes keeping tabs on me.

"Any luck?" Tania asked as I walked in.

"I don't know. It took me a bunch of places that weren't helpful," I answered, throwing myself onto the couch beside her. Maggie was nowhere to be seen.

"Maybe we can figure out a pattern?" the older woman offered.

"I don't know. It took me to the police station and the B&B which I guess makes sense. It was tracking itself rather than whoever had left behind the blood stain. But then at the B&B I managed to do ... well I'm not really sure what, but it supercharged the vine and actually went looking for the killer. But it took me to Tyson's and then out of town."

"You think whoever it was fled?"

"I don't know. When I talked to Walter earlier, he seemed like he was going to come to the service. At least I thought I'd convinced him to come. He said he was staying at the hotel Chief Hayes had offered to pay for us. I don't know where Vera's fiancé has been staying. The spot looked like someone had gotten in a car and left in a hurry."

"Would either of them have any other reason to stick around besides the service?"

One of them could have the money. But I knew for a fact neither of them had her ring. "The ring. Walter mentioned she had some of his mother's jewelry. He didn't mention the ring specifically, but it could fit. And if I were her fiancé and she's run off with an expensive ring, I'd stick around until I found it, too."

"So, maybe the vine was showing you places the killer had been after all?"

"Yeah, but I still don't know if that means her fiancé or Walter."

Tania nodded slowly. "We have to assume that Rick has the killer's DNA. But processing it and things like fingerprints does take a few days around here. We've got outdated technology."

It also explained why I still hadn't heard back on that blood sample I'd given. Sinking against the pillows I frowned at Tania.

She tilted her head to one side. "So, what are you going to do now?"

"I'm not going to just give up. There has to be another way to figure out if it's one of the two of them."

Unfortunately, that way was eluding me. Maybe some more sleep would illuminate things. After all, tomorrow was Vera's memorial service, and the clock was ticking to get Chief Hayes to believe I hadn't been involved.

19

I woke to the sound of my phone skittering across the bedside table. I blindly grabbed for it, sending it clattering to the floor in my stupor. Groaning, I blinked the sleep from my eyes and bent over the side of the bed to retrieve my phone. It had a text from Sage that displayed on my phone's locked screen.

'Meet at High Time in one hour.'

Blood pounded in my ears. Why did she want to meet in an hour? As far as I knew the service for Vera wasn't until late morning. I tapped the message to open it in the app to find that she'd sent the message to everyone on the staff group message. It wasn't just me. She probably just wanted help setting everything up.

Laying back against the pillows, I let my heart rate return to normal. Even with the close distance between Maggie's flat and High Time, I didn't have time to lay about. I rooted around in the bag I'd packed to find clean clothes. I picked out a dark blue top and beige capris. It wasn't exactly funeral attire, but it would have to do.

I emerged a few minutes later, twisting a few curly strands of hair out of my face to find Maggie sitting at the kitchen table lost in thought.

"Morning," I greeted, approaching the coffee pot to her left.

"You're up early," she noted.

"Sage wants everyone to come in early. I guess to help set up for the service."

"You were right," she said after a moment of silence.

"About what?" I poured the last remnants of the current pot into a cup. I might have to stop by Ginny's for a proper cup on my way in.

"I went back through the inventory last night. There was some healing balm missing. And I checked the register and there wasn't any record of a transaction."

"What if they paid cash?"

She shook her head. "If they'd paid for it, it would have been logged in the system."

She hadn't gotten back before I'd gone to bed the night before, so I hadn't had a chance to fill her in on what I'd learned from my little magical trip around town. "I almost found the killer. Except I think they might be trying to leave town and I still can't be sure who it actually is."

"That doesn't bode well. Rick hates unsolved cases more than he hates people committing crimes in his town."

I took note of that statement and filed it away for later. "I need to find a way to get whoever it is to come back to town. I need to know what happened to her."

"But if he's left, how are you supposed to do that?"

"I have no idea," I groaned, setting the now empty mug on the counter in front of me. "Do you have any suggestions?"

"No. Except, whatever you do end up doing, please be careful and bring someone with a heartbeat as back-up this time. Maybe someone with a badge and gun."

I gave a soft snort. "I will try."

"You better get to High Time. You don't want to be late," she said, nudging my shoulder with hers.

I didn't argue. Instead, I left the comfort of her home behind and stepped into the early morning air. I couldn't shake the sense of foreboding hanging over me as I walked up Main Street. I was trying to put myself in the path of a killer. A man who hadn't thought twice about murder or violating another person's privacy by breaking into their home. Before I'd come here, I never would have done something so dangerous. So, why was I doing it now?

Because if I didn't, I would have to live with the stigma of people thinking I'd had a hand in her death somehow. And I couldn't handle that. Still, I couldn't ignore the tiny voice in the back of my head accusing me of just wanting to be a hero so people would like me. I hadn't been unpopular back home, but the residents of Brookhaven didn't have a reason to like me or trust me especially with me being an outsider. If I solved this case, it would go a long way toward earning some good will.

I stayed stuck in my thoughts until I reached the lot behind High Time. A few other employees milled about, looking tired. Only then did I realize I'd meant to stop at Ginny's for a pick-me-up.

"Thanks for coming guys," Sage called, carrying

a travel carafe of coffee and some paper cups as she approached.

My eyes lit up at the promise of caffeine and I saw a few other people straighten, too. Sage led us inside to the break room where she'd set up a small table offering pastries and muffins, too. I waited until she'd set down the coffee and cups before pouring myself some and taking an apple pastry then stepped back to stand by my locker. I saw Thomas across the way nursing a cup of coffee, too. He kept glancing at the food and then away.

"Okay everyone, so I first wanted to say thanks to everyone who came to me asking to organize the service this afternoon for Vera. I know she wasn't part of our family long, but she was still one of us," Sage began.

A few employees glanced in my direction with not so friendly looks. Everyone knew I'd found her, and they probably also knew what Chief Hayes thought I'd done. They all knew my job here and even if the weapon of choice hadn't been publicly disclosed, I had little doubt someone had caught a glimpse as the coroner removed her body. I tried to let the accusatory glances roll off me as I focused on Sage and her instructions for later in the day.

"So, for those of you who haven't been involved

in all the planning, we're going to head to the pier at ten. Then set up chairs and a table with a guest book for folks to sign. The service will start at eleven."

"Who is going to be speaking?" one of the cooks in the back asked.

"Whoever feels like they've got something to say," Sage answered.

Holding the service on the pier wasn't a bad idea. It could accommodate lots of people and take advantage of the nice weather and the serene view of the water. And it was a place I knew Walter had been. That still didn't help me get him or Vera's fiancé there by eleven though.

"Oh, we'll be closed all weekend to honor Vera's memory," Sage noted as her phone pinged with an incoming message. She glanced at the screen and then said, "Okay, chairs were just dropped off. Can those of you with cars come help bring them down to the pier?"

A few people murmured their assent before tossing their empty coffee cups in the trash and heading for the front of the shop. Before long, Thomas and I stood alone in the break room, eying each other over the leftover muffins.

"You not going to help?" he asked.

"Don't have a car," I reminded him. "You?"

"Yeah. I'll go over in a bit to help unload."

"You alright, mate?" I noted. He still looked nervous as he shifted his weight from one foot to the other. Not quite rocking in place, but certainly a mark of someone who was not comfortable in the space they were in. One might even say suspicious.

"It's stupid. I just keep thinking about the fact I thought she had a weird sense of humor the last time I saw her."

"Not to her face, you didn't," I reminded.

"Still, I said it and I thought it too. Now someone's gone and killed her and I just feel terrible."

I rounded the table and put a hand on his shoulder. "Don't. Nothing you said or did is the reason she's not here right now."

He gave me a somber smile. "Thanks. And look at me, being such a mess when we all know you were brought in to talk to the chief."

"Nothing I can't handle," I said, trying to convince myself as much as my co-worker. I felt my phone buzz in my pocket, but I didn't move to check it.

Thomas let out a long exhale and cleared his throat. "I'm going to head over. See you there?"

"Yeah." I glanced around the break room. "I'm just going to clean this up first."

Sage would appreciate the assistance after emceeing the service and I needed the privacy to look at whatever had just come through on my phone. I saw a missed call from Tania with a notification that she'd left a voicemail. I set the phone on the table, put it on speaker and started clearing the detritus into a trash bin.

"Hi, it's Tania. You probably saw that from the Caller ID. Never mind. I wanted to remind you that you had some spare phones somewhere and didn't want you to forget about them in case you needed them. I'll see you at the service."

I stared at my phone in confusion.

"Spare phones?" I murmured.

Vera's hidden stash!

I was such an idiot. I'd come in the other day intent on figuring out how to access them and I'd stowed them in my locker, because Sage had been here and distracted me with the video footage.

I fumbled the locker door open and groped around on the top shelf where I'd stored them under the extra work shirt. For a moment, my heart stopped beating, because I couldn't find them. Then, my finger brushed something hard and rectangular.

I stuffed the phones and the shirt under my arm. I picked up my phone and hit Sage's number on speed dial.

"Everything okay Darcy?" Sage sounded out of breath.

"Yeah, uh Tania was going to make some food for afterward and she's called with a bit of an emergency. Is it okay if I go help? I'll be there before everything starts."

"Yeah, I think I've got enough hands."

I ended the call and darted out the back of the shop. I had phones to unlock.

I MADE IT AS FAR AS THE HIGH TIME PARKING LOT before I stopped short. I was not even remotely close to being a tech whiz. I was lucky I didn't forget my phone's password half the time. There was no way I was going to be able to unlock Vera's phones in the next two hours. The weight of the pilfered phones was noticeable beneath my arm as I consulted my own phone. There had to be a reason Tania had called and left me the message now. I hit redial and waited as the line rang.

"Did you get my message?"

"I did. I've got them, but I've no idea what to do with them now." After a beat, I added, "I didn't really think it through when I found them."

"Bring them here," I heard Maggie's voice on the other end of the line.

"And do what with them?"

"Just bring them," she said.

"You should listen to her," Tania said.

"Okay. See you in a few minutes," I answered and ended the call.

I found them both standing in the living room, eyes glued to the front door as I came in. Maggie advanced on me and held out her hand.

"Let me see them."

"What are you going to do with them? I don't think you can heal technology."

She laughed and pointed to a laptop set up on the coffee table next to the couch. "I'm not going to be doing magic. Not unless you consider a little light hacking to be supernatural."

I stared at her in disbelief, my jaw going slack. Maggie had given me flack for snagging the piece of vine and yet here she was, ready to break into another person's phone without permission. I couldn't decide if this revelation annoyed or impressed me. Maybe a little of both.

"I don't know which is which."

"It won't matter unless I can get them unlocked." Maggie sat on the couch, pulling the laptop onto her knees. She plugged the first phone into a cord and tapped away at the keys on the computer.

The lock screen lit up with an image of fireworks over water. Not remotely helpful in determining if this was Vera's phone, or her McKenzie identity. She did the same with the second phone. It had a generic lock screen image that had probably come with the phone. Also, not helpful.

"Okay, let's try her birthday," Maggie said, waving her hand at me as if I was supposed to hand her something.

I scrambled for my own phone and pulled up Vera's profile first. "Uh, Vera's says 17 May."

I watched as Maggie keyed 0517 into both phones. It did nothing to unlock either. "Try switching it around, so it's day then month," I suggested.

Her brow furrowed as she entered 1705 with similar failed results. So, she hadn't used her birthday. I switched over to McKenzie's profile to see that it showed a different birthday. "Try 7 June."

Maggie keyed in 0607 and nothing happened. Her frustration intensified and her cheeks flushed as she tried 0706 without luck. "I'm only going to have one more shot at this before they both become bricks."

"You could try 1-2-3-4," I suggested.

"Not funny," Maggie muttered.

I navigated back to Vera's page and scrolled through, trying to find any other numbers that might be relevant. Nothing seemed obvious and McKenzie's page was even less forthcoming. But Vera had an active Instagram until recently. I scrolled through those photos, looking for anything that might signal an important date in her life. An anniversary ... *something*.

"I don't know if it's worth trying, but what about 12 July?"

"Where did that come from?" Tania interjected.

I held up my phone so she could see the date on the engagement ring post. "For all I know she posted it weeks after it happened, but it's all I've got."

Maggie keyed in 0712 into the second phone and it came up with another wrong password attempt before it went dark. My gut clenched as she moved to the first phone. My palms turned sweaty as I waited for her to try the combination. Her hand moved in slow motion and my heart leapt into my throat. My vision tunneled as she tapped the display.

The fireworks disappeared, replaced by a bright sunset background and cluttered home screen of apps. I blinked, not believing it had actually worked. I snatched the phone off the cord and started tapping buttons, opening the address book. None of the names meant anything to me and my heart sank when I got to the 'L's and Walter's name wasn't there. I scrolled down to the end of the list, but she had no contacts under 'W' either. The 'B's, for 'brother' or 'big bro' were equally missing. Maybe she had deleted his number from her contacts if they'd had a falling out? Unfortunately, I still didn't know her fiancé's name. She hadn't tagged him in any of her photos.

There was an unread text message notification when I closed out of the contacts. I opened it to find a number not associated with a contact from the list. It went back a few weeks. The most recent message was from the day before Vera was killed.

'You can't hide from me forever.'

I looked back through the short thread to find that Vera had not texted the number back except at the very start to tell the number to leave her alone. Had this been how Walter, or her fiancé found her? I left the app and went searching through the phone's settings, but nothing jumped out at me, signaling someone had been able to track her phone.

"So, now what?" Tania prodded.

A plan was taking root in my mind. It was a terrible idea, but it was all I had.

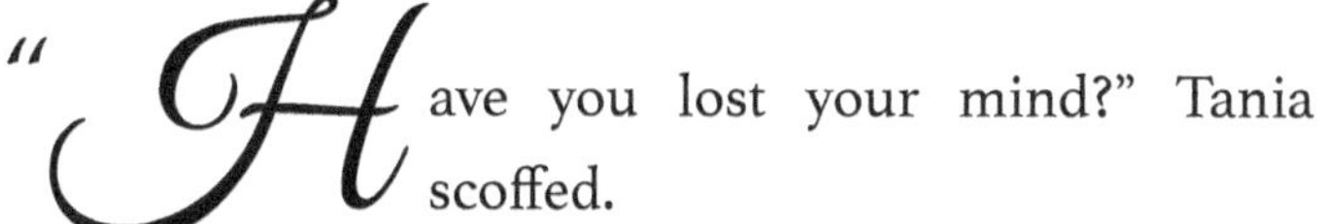

20

"Have you lost your mind?" Tania scoffed.

"No," I retorted. "We need whoever sent that message to come back to town so that Chief Hayes can arrest him. Sending him a text could do just that." I could call the number too. I'd heard both men's voices, but I didn't want to give away it was me on the other end.

"I'm inclined to agree with Tania," Maggie said when I turned to look at her for support. "It's pretty clear she told whoever was sending those messages to leave her alone. She hasn't responded since. If all of a sudden she was to send a text, it would be suspicious."

"Especially since she's dead!" Tania interjected.

"But he has to know someone has the ring. Either me or the police. If he really wants that back, he might just be desperate enough to come looking for it."

"And what are you going to do if he actually does show up?" Tania challenged.

"Get him to confess to what he did so Chief Hayes knows he got the right guy," I said.

"Darcy, you are talking about luring in a killer," Maggie pointed out quietly.

"I am not going to go alone," I said, eying her.

"I think we should hand the phones and the ring over to the police. Let them decide what to do with it," Tania said.

"I can't just drop it now." I reached out a hand to catch her by the wrist. "Please, you pushed me to investigate the hit and run back when we first met. Why should this be any different?"

"Because no one got seriously hurt then. It was missing money. Not dead bodies," she answered, throwing her hands up in the air and dislodging my grasp.

I couldn't argue with her point. It had felt like far lower stakes when it was missing money instead of a killer on the loose. But I needed to see this through.

"Look, you don't have to be involved at all. I can do this on my own."

"You're not facing a killer by yourself. Besides, you might need medical attention," Maggie said and crossed her arms over her chest. "If you're dead set on doing this insane plan, I'm going with you."

I glanced back at Tania. "Do you think Vinnie would let us do this with his blessing?"

"Vinnie's not the one you need to win over," she answered.

There was no chance in hell I'd get the chief to agree to something like this. But Vinnie might be more willing to back me up. "He would probably be unhappy about keeping it from Rick," Maggie said.

"What if we alert them to what's going on right before it happens? That way we can be sure they're present and they can hear everything?" I offered.

"Rick would still be furious with you," Tania said pointedly.

"Yeah, but he'd also have a killer in custody."

"Ooh, I get a conspiratorial vibe in here," Sam said, revealing his presence as he floated through the front door.

Maggie glared at him. "I know Tania and Darcy are currently without a residence, but you are perfectly welcome to stay there."

"Missed you, too," he said and blew her a kiss. "But really, what are you ladies chatting about?"

"Maggie got Vera's phone unlocked. It looks like the killer was texting her. I think I might be able to get him to come back to town and hopefully get him to confess," I answered in one long breath.

"You do not do things small, do you?" he noted.

"Would appear that way," I answered.

There was no point in sitting around debating the decision. It would either work or it wouldn't. Either way, nothing would happen if I didn't take the leap and send the text.

"Tania, where did you put the ring?" I needed to make sure I had proof that I had the item in question. Just saying I did wouldn't be enough.

"I really don't like this," she muttered, but disappeared into Maggie's bedroom. She reappeared a minute later with the ring.

I took it and laid it on the living room table in front of me. On closer inspection, it didn't seem as gaudy as I'd initially thought. I picked up the phone we'd unlocked and snapped a photo of the ring. My mouth went dry as I opened the text chain and typed a message.

'I think I've got something of yours.'

I waited for a response. Before I realized it, both

Maggie and Tania flanked me on the couch and Sam hovered in the middle of the table. All of our gazes were glued to the screen. This had to work. It was the only play I had left.

Finally, three little dots appeared showing the other number was composing a message.

'Who is this?'

I wasn't about to tell him who I was. Instead, I forwarded the image of the ring and waited. The response came faster this time.

'That isn't yours.'

"He isn't the brightest bulb is he?" Sam commented.

"Where are you going to tell him to meet you? It should be somewhere public," Maggie prompted.

Part of me wanted to do it at High Time where all of this had started. The pier was too public for what I wanted to do.

'Meet me after her service.'

'Where?'

'Where she died.'

I couldn't explain why, but sending that last text made my nerves jangle and I tossed the phone aside. There was no backing out now. I pointed from the phone to Tania and back. "We don't need it anymore. You can turn it into the police."

"And what should I tell Rick about where I found it?"

I was about to suggest that Sage found them while cleaning out Vera's locker, but I couldn't throw my boss under the bus like that. "I don't know. Tell them the truth that I found them."

"I just hope you two don't get yourselves killed," she muttered and scooped up both phones and stowed them in her purse. She stopped by the kitchen table to gather up some trays of chocolate-covered marzipan she'd prepared. I hadn't entirely lied to Sage about Tania needing help with food. "Now come on, we're going to be late for the service.

I pocketed the ring as I followed her and Maggie out of the flat. Time to catch a killer.

21

*S*age had woefully underestimated the number of chairs for the service. The entirety of Brookhaven had turned out to mourn the loss of one of its newest residents.

"I almost wish I get this kind of reception when I die," I murmured to Maggie.

I caught Sam flickering into existence and glowering at the crowd. I didn't bother asking why he was so out of sorts and Maggie didn't offer up an explanation if she knew it. I spotted the rest of the employees from High Time up front huddled together. I knew I should go sit with them, but being in the back of the crowd allowed me a bit of anonymity and the ability to look for Walter or Vera's fiancé.

It was easier said than done thanks to the fact that while Brookhaven was a small town, it was still populated enough to have several hundred people. I couldn't hope to go through every face in the time I had.

"You told him to meet you after the service. Relax," Maggie said and patted my knee.

"I don't need him lying in wait for me there. I picked it so that I could hopefully control what happened."

"You have to know people will notice if you leave early," she reminded me.

"Not if I'm with Beau."

She shook her head and turned back to watching the last few stragglers come up the boardwalk. Maybe I was using Beau as a crutch, but a girl had to use whatever assets were available to her. It wasn't my fault he had a really useful power that came in handy more than my own magic.

I did one last review of the crowd as Sage stepped up to a podium. A large poster sized picture of Vera's ID photo sat off to her left. I spotted Vinnie and Chief Hayes off to one side, doing their best to act as crowd control. Tania sat two seats down from me and she kept eying the officers. She no doubt wanted to pass along the evidence. As I turned to survey the back of the assembled crowd, I spotted Walter off to one side. His eyes were bloodshot and he kept his hands shoved in his pockets. I turned the other way and spotted Vera's fiancé, too. *Which of them did I text?* The crackle of a microphone squealed, pulling my focus to the front of the assembly like a magnet.

"Thank you all for coming." Sage's voice wavered. Even from this distance I could see the stress pinching the corners of her eyes and mouth. Her usually vibrant blue eyes were watery with unshed tears. "It warms me to see so many people turn out to celebrate the life of one of Brookhaven's newest additions. We wanted to use this time to let anyone who would like to share their thoughts or memories of Vera speak."

"I hope people talk," I whispered.

To my surprise, Thomas was first up to the podium when Sage stepped away. I suppose this was one way to assuage his guilt. "I didn't know Vera well, but she was a welcome change to our little ecosystem at High Time. She had a quirky sense of humor and it made me laugh. I wish I'd gotten a chance to know her better. She seemed like a kind person with a good heart." He glanced at the photo. "You will be missed."

I tuned out as other people got up and offered brief remarks. I wondered if anyone expected Tania or I to go up and say something, but it was like Beau's invisibility had already fallen over me. No one paid me any mind. Except, I could still feel someone's gaze on me. With both men at the back of the crowd, it could have been either one. I didn't want to give them the satisfaction of knowing it bothered me, so I stayed facing forward.

When no one else moved to share their thoughts, Sage returned to the podium to say, "Let's have a moment of silence in remembrance."

Even though no one else had been speaking, a hush fell over the crowd. It didn't seem possible for a group this large outside on the water to be capable of such silence and yet it was almost deafening. Finally, the microphone squawked again as Sage said, "There will be some light refreshments outside of Ginny's."

My heart had stopped beating for a moment until she'd finished her sentence. For a moment I'd feared she was going to send everyone back to the dispensary and ruin my plan to confront Vera's killer. Speaking of, when I turned back to check the crowd as it dispersed, I didn't see either Walter or her fiancé.

"Come on. We need to go," I told Maggie and slid into the next group of people leaving their seats behind. I didn't check to see if Tania had watched us go, or if she was with the police. Beau appeared on a vacant cart as we approached Main Street and I picked him up. We moved with determination to High Time, arriving before the first wave of people had even reached Ginny's. The parking lot was empty and yet I could feel a presence lurking.

"Give me your phone," Maggie said, holding out her hand.

I didn't question her request as I passed it over. "Keep Maggie safe," I whispered and passed the reptile to my friend. I watched as the pair of them shimmered and blended in with the surrounding greenery.

"I know you're here," I called and produced the ring, lifting it up so he could see it from whatever vantage point he had.

"Hand it over," a voice demanded. It was *not* Walter's.

From out of the shadow of the side of the building, Vera's fiancé appeared. The way he sauntered toward me turned my stomach.

"You?" I couldn't hide the confusion in my voice.

"Look, my beef isn't with you. Give me that ring and we never have to see each other again."

"Not until you tell me why you did it," I blurted. I had no intention of giving him the ring.

"Excuse me?" He pulled out a knife, flicking the blade open with an audible 'snick.' The movement was enough to draw my attention to his hands. They were devoid of marks, but I caught a scratch on his forearm that could have come from Vera if she'd fought him off.

I took a step back, my palms growing sweaty in fear. *'Please tell me the police are here,'* I thought as loudly as I could to Beau.

'Listening.'

Beau's confirmation was enough to force the lump out of my throat with as much confidence as I could muster, I said, "You want the ring, you tell me why she had to die."

"You are one nosy little ... you know what? Fine. She took what was mine and I wanted it back."

"The money," I replied.

"She thought she could just decide to leave me and take the money *I* worked for."

"That's why she was running, because she stole your money and dumped you?"

"You don't miss a thing do you," he scoffed.

"So that meant she had to die?"

"She knew what she did and what the punishment was."

"Punishment? She was a human being. You don't get to be the arbiter of her life."

"When you're with Maxwell Fontaine, you know what that means. She signed up for this. She didn't just get to walk away."

His name meant nothing to me, but the way he talked about her like property made my blood boil. They might have looked happy on the surface, but Vera had been involved with an abuser. I hadn't even noticed the signs. Not before it was too late anyway.

"Why the vine?" I probed. "Why go to all that trouble to use a vine?"

He let out a snigger. "Because a little birdie told me that you were new in town, too and you liked plants. No one knew I was here, but you two were staying in the same place. You were working together. Cute, she thought she could go from working for me to selling product for someone else and I wouldn't notice."

Product?

Suddenly the hundred thousand dollars made sense. She'd stolen drug money. It still didn't answer the question of why Walter was in town or why Vera denied knowing him. "How does Walter fit into all of this?"

"Who's Walter?" he scoffed.

"Her brother. He's been looking for her for months. Was it your idea or hers to cut ties with her family? To lie about who she was? Or did you find out she wasn't who you thought she was. Is that why she really ran from you?"

Max shook his head, gripping the knife loosely in his left hand. "I don't know what you're talking about. She's dead, because she stole my money and that ring. And if you don't want to end up the same, you'll give me that ring and let me walk away."

"You can't really think I'm going to let you take this and leave," I replied with more confidence than I actually felt.

Time slowed as he lunged for me. All I could see was the cold metal of the blade as it inched closer to my belly. In that moment, I was back in my head in that space where the seedling of my magic grew.

"I need you," I whispered.

Where before it had only a few leaves and the beginnings of petals, it now burst forth with slithering vines and thorns of its own. They shot forth from the cracks in the pavement, twisting around his wrists and ankles, holding him fast.

"What the!" he howled.

Thorns bit into his exposed flesh hard enough to draw blood and he dropped the knife.

"Stop, police!" Chief Hayes called from behind me.

I stepped back from him and held my hands where the chief could see them. He came abreast with me, gun aimed firmly at Max. He glanced at me and said, "The next time you decide to go rogue, I'm going to arrest you, Miss Ingram."

"Understood."

"You are very lucky you have a landlady who I happen to be fond of," he added.

I heard shoes scuff on the ground. Maggie and Beau became visible again. She held up her phone which showed an active call with Tania. My phone was aimed at Max with a video still recording. They'd both had my back after all.

"So, you heard everything?" I addressed the chief as Vinnie moved in with cuffs.

"We did." He holstered his weapon. "Would you mind releasing my suspect?"

Embarrassment flushed my cheeks. "Right. Sorry, Vinnie."

I held up my hands and envisioned the vines snaking back into the earth, ready to aid me again some time. To my surprise they did exactly as I wanted, save for one thorn that remained lodged in Max's upper arm. Retribution for using it to kill Vera perhaps. Vinnie cuffed Max and Chief Hayes dragged him off toward Main Street and the station.

Vinnie stopped beside me. "You should know we finally got the DNA results and you weren't a match. We also found traces of gamma hydroxybutyrate known as GHB in your blood, a date rape drug. You were right, you were drugged. Sorry we hounded you."

"You were doing your job," I said, although I appreciated the apology. It would have meant more coming from Chief Hayes, but I'd take what I could get.

As I turned to follow him out of the lot, I spotted Walter standing on the sidewalk, having watched the scene with Max unfold. I realized now that the text exchange I'd had was with Max, not Walter. But he'd come back and was sticking around. That was a mystery for another day.

22

I stared at the headline of the Brookhaven Gazette on Monday morning as I sipped coffee from one of the oversized mugs at Ginny's. I didn't know what Chief Hayes had on the town's local paper to keep them from printing the article sooner. The article took up the entire front page of the paper. Gerry would have been pleased I'd picked up a physical copy.

Will the Real Vera Chase Please Stand Up?
By: Francine Baylor

Less than a week ago, the heinous murder of newcomer Vera Chase disrupted Brookhaven's tranquility. For days, people questioned why someone would want to harm the woman most of them hardly knew. After all, things like this don't happen in our sleepy little town.

But there was more to Vera Chase than met the eye. A troubled past forced her to flee to Brookhaven seeking sanctuary. According to her co-workers at High Time, she had been in a bad relationship and was looking to start over. What she failed to mention is that the bad relationship was with notorious New York drug dealer Maxwell Fontaine. Fontaine is suspected of several crimes including manufacturing and possession with intent to distribute. According to sources in the New York City Police Department, who commented on condition of anonymity, no charges have been formally brought against Fontaine at this time.

So, the question remains: who was the real Vera Chase? Local proprietor Tyson Samuels offered up one theory. "I think she got greedy and saw an opportunity to make some quick cash and it caught up with her." One of her co-workers, Thomas Fuller urged respect for the dead, "Whoever she was before she came here, she was a decent person. No matter what she did in her past, no one deserves what happened to her."

As usual, Brookhaven's Chief of Police Rick Hayes is tight-lipped on his investigation, although he has confirmed that evidence obtained at the scene ties Fontaine to Chase's death.

"Anything good in there?" Maggie asked as she sat down on the other side of the booth.

"Not really. There's got to be more to the story than what was printed and what Max raved about on Saturday. I mean, they didn't even talk about the other identity. I still don't get how it all fits together," I replied and set the paper aside.

Maggie leaned across the table. "Well, I heard Chief Hayes interrogating him while I was giving my statement. And he swore up and down he had no idea who McKenzie Lawson was." She drummed her fingers on the table. "I may have also seen some information on his computer that said McKenzie Lawson has different fingerprints than Vera."

I gaped at her. "What? Are you sure?"

"It was quick, but yeah, it looks like they were two different people."

Why hadn't that occurred to me? It was a much simpler answer than her having two identities. They had different birthdays, even their online personas from the little I had gathered diverged. Vera had been more outgoing while McKenzie was more subdued. Which meant that Walter had been wrong about Vera being his sister. Which begged a new question: where was McKenzie?

"But Walter was sure that Vera was McKenzie. How could that happen?"

Maggie shrugged. "Don't they say that everyone has a doppelganger out there somewhere? It wouldn't surprise me that Brookhaven attracted a pair. And if he only interacted with Vera once, it was possible he was so desperate to find his sister that he believed it was her, even if all signs pointed to that not being the case."

"You really think they somehow ran into each other? And what, Vera somehow took McKenzie's ID and phone by mistake?"

Maggie shook her head. "Given what she was running from, I would guess she took them on purpose. For all we know they rode out of New York on the same bus."

"I wish I could ask Vera what happened. But as far as I know, no one in this town talks to the dead. At least not ones without ghosts."

"We are short on necromancers, I'm afraid," she agreed.

We fell silent as I set aside the paper and studied the contents of my mug. Before long, a shadow fell over the rim and I looked up to see Ginny standing there, looking uncomfortable. She was off her usual perch.

"I owe you an apology," she said through gritted teeth.

"What for?" Across the booth, Maggie settled back, as if to watch a show. Or maybe a sparring match.

"I may have ... told that psycho that you had a thing for plants."

"Excuse me?" I couldn't have heard her right. Had she just told me she'd pointed Max in my direction?

"He was new in town and obviously I make it my business to find out what I can about anyone passing through. He was asking if anyone knew who'd come through lately and I may have let slip that you were new and had a thing with plants." She made a wiping motion, as if none of what she'd just said was really important. "I suppose I shouldn't have told him that because he sort of framed you and you could have gone to jail. I'm sorry." The last word came out through gritted teeth.

I wasn't even surprised. I should have assumed

Ginny had a hand in landing me at the center of her brother's investigation. It did unnerve me a little that she'd shared any information about me, no matter how truthful, with a stranger.

"I get you want to protect the reputation of the town, but I have literally done nothing to you, Ginny. Not a bloody thing."

Ginny turned her nose up and marched away without another word. Maggie snorted in reaction. "One day she will stop trying to control everything and everyone around her and we will all be better for it."

"But today is not that day," I told her.

The tiny bell above the door jangled and Walter appeared. Our gazes met and he did an about face, disappearing from view. He owed me answers. I left Maggie sitting in the booth and went after him.

'Pier.'

I spotted Beau lounging on a bench outside Ginny's before he faded into the woodwork. "Thanks."

It wasn't hard to find Walter, even with the boardwalk bustling with daytime foot traffic. He had stopped at the spot we'd held Vera's memorial. Even though it hadn't been his sister we'd laid to rest, clearly he'd still felt a connection.

"I'm sorry," I said as I approached him.

"You didn't do anything," he said.

"I kind of spent the last week thinking you could have been a killer," I admitted.

"Guess we were both fooled by mistaken identity," he said with a bitter laugh.

"At least now we know that Vera and McKenzie are two different people. That means your sister could still be out there, Walter."

"It explains why I could still feel her," he murmured.

"Can I ask why she ran away?"

"I pushed her," he answered, tears welling in his eyes. "She started showing signs of ... a certain family trait. I pushed too hard. She got scared and took off. I've been trying to find her ever since."

"Would that family trait happen to be spelled m-a-g-i-c?"

Color drained from his cheeks. "Um ..."

"It's okay. Pretty much everyone in this place is in the know."

"I suspected when I saw you do that thing with the plants," he said.

I was still amazed I'd managed to do something akin to real magic with my powers to defend myself and Maggie. "If your sister is still out there, I want to help you find her."

"You don't have to do that."

"Yes, I do. I spent the last week thinking your sister was dead and that I'd somehow been part of the cause. Finding her alive now, getting to meet her. That would give me closure."

Besides, I owed it to Walter to help track McKenzie down. I'd misjudged him and I wasn't going to make that mistake again. Vera's murder might have been solved, but there was still one more loose end to tie up.

Wherever you are McKenzie, I am going to find you.

QUICK AUTHOR'S NOTE

I WILL ADMIT, IT TOOK ME A LONG TIME TO FIND Darcy's voice. I knew her story was going to be full of magic and discovery, in part because I love that fantastical element and I knew that's what I was meant to write. And, I was super excited to give her some fun sidekicks in Beau and Sam. Who doesn't love a quirky ghost and an unusual familiar?

I do hope you enjoyed Darcy's first full-length adventure in Brookhaven, as it is not going to be her last. Far from it, in fact! This series is going to be one of the longest I've ever done. We're going to get to share in some big moments for Darcy. After all, she's got to learn to use her powers someday, right? And if you haven't gotten a chance to read about Darcy's first visit to Brookhaven, stick around because I've got a special offer just for you!

Where will her snooping take her next? Well, as you saw from the end of this book, there's still the mystery of where is McKenzie Lawson? I think you're going to really enjoy what is coming next for Darcy and company. I hadn't planned on having a story that bled so directly through one book to the next, but as I was writing *High Noon*, it just felt right.

TURN THE PAGE TO GET A GLIMPSE AT *HIGH TIDE*...

<u>HIGH TIDE</u>

Time and tide wait for no witch

Darcy Ingram's time in supernaturally-tinged Brookhaven has been anything but idyllic. She solved one murder, but now a friend begs her to help find his missing sister. A day cruise with her co-workers sounds like just the break she needs. But when a passenger dies under unusual circumstances. she finds herself tangled up in another mystery.

Darcy's snooping suggests her missing person may be involved, but as she unearths more clues about the victim's life, she's left with more questions and a growing list of suspects.

With the help of her friends and her blossoming plant magic. Darcy uncovers the killer. But will her power be enough to save her friend's life and stop the killer in their tracks?

Scan QR code to buy High Tide today

ABOUT THE AUTHOR

S.E. Biglow is the pen name of *USA Today* bestselling author Sarah Biglow. She lives in Massachusetts with her husband and son. She is a licensed attorney and spends her days combatting employment discrimination as an Investigator with the Massachusetts Commission Against Discrimination.

You can find an up-to-date list of all my books here